HAZU~

THE GUILD MEMBER WITH A **WORTHLESS SKILL** IS ACTUALLY A **LEGENDARY ASSASSIN**

Kennoji

ILLUSTRATION BY KWKM

Roland Argan

The former legendary assassin who killed the demon lord. He now is a guild employee seeking a normal life.

Rileyla Diakitep

Former demon lord and currently Roland's demonic lover. Nicknamed Rila. She's grown attached to Roland and lives with him.

Candice Minelad

A vampire who used to be part of the demon lord's army that Rila led. Currently an adventurer.

Roje Sandsong

An elf who used to be part of the demon lord's army that Rila led. A remarkable mage and Rila's loyal retainer.

Iris Negan

The manager of the Lahti branch, where Roland works. She is one of the few, apart from the guild master, who knows Roland's true identity.

Milia McGuffin

Guild receptionist. She trained Roland and is the most uplifting presence at the Lahti branch.

"Who do you think an assassin kills first?"

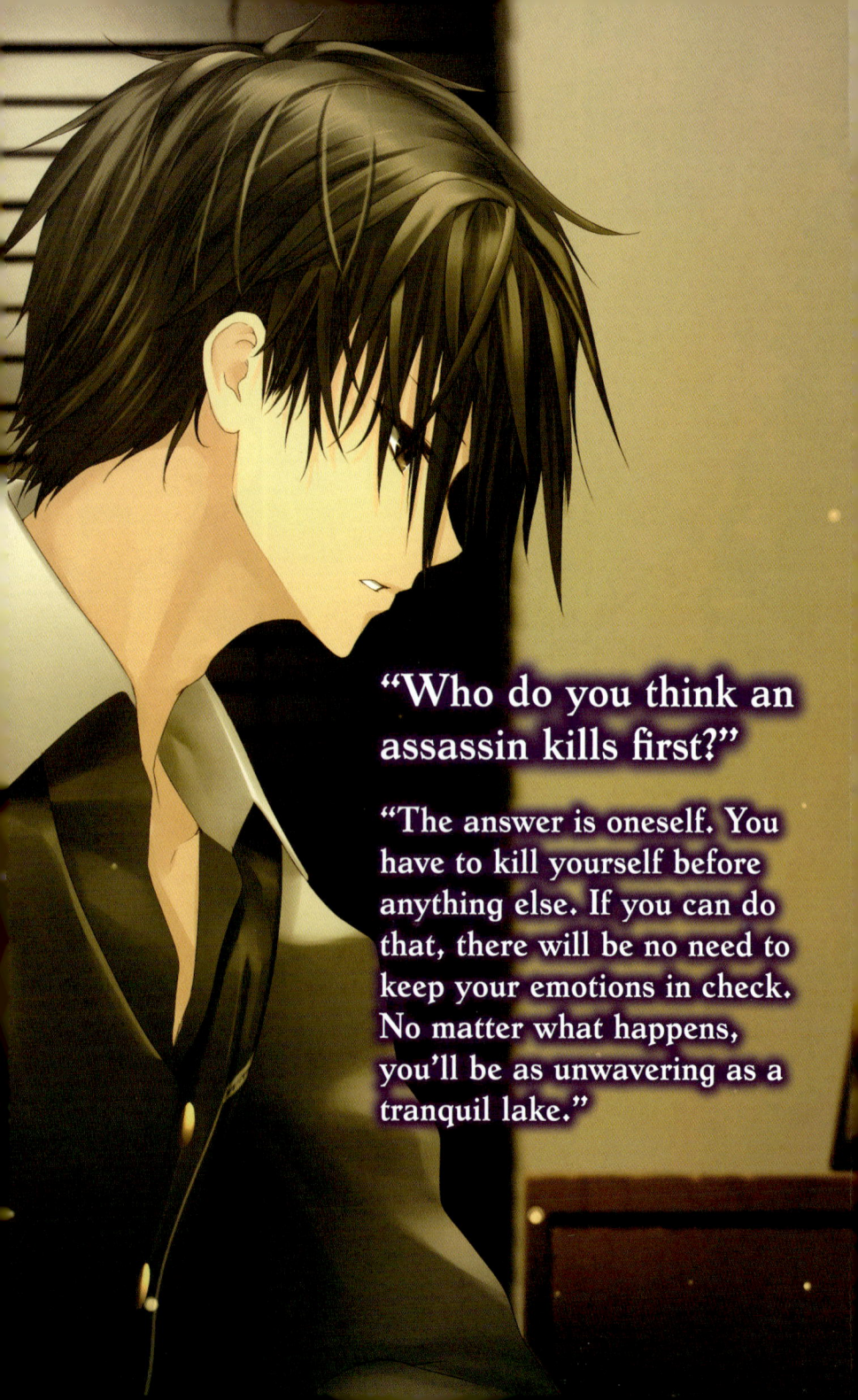

"The answer is oneself. You have to kill yourself before anything else. If you can do that, there will be no need to keep your emotions in check. No matter what happens, you'll be as unwavering as a tranquil lake."

HAZURE SKILL
THE GUILD MEMBER WITH A WORTHLESS SKILL IS ACTUALLY A LEGENDARY ASSASSIN

4

Kennoji

ILLUSTRATION BY
KWKM

YEN ON
New York

Hazure Skill: The Guild Member with a Worthless Skill Is Actually a Legendary Assassin, Vol. 4
Kennoji

Translation by Jan Mitsuko Cash
Cover art by KWKM

This book is a work of fiction. Names, characters, places, and incidents are the product of the author's imagination or are used fictitiously. Any resemblance to actual events, locales, or persons, living or dead, is coincidental.

HAZURE SKILL "KAGE GA USUI" WO MOTSU GUILD SHOKUIN GA, JITSU WA DENSETSU NO ANSATSUSHA Vol. 4
©Kennoji, KWKM, 2020
First published in Japan in 2020 by KADOKAWA CORPORATION, Tokyo.
English translation rights arranged with KADOKAWA CORPORATION, Tokyo through TUTTLE-MORI AGENCY, INC., Tokyo.

English translation © 2022 by Yen Press, LLC

Yen Press, LLC supports the right to free expression and the value of copyright. The purpose of copyright is to encourage writers and artists to produce the creative works that enrich our culture.

The scanning, uploading, and distribution of this book without permission is a theft of the author's intellectual property. If you would like permission to use material from the book (other than for review purposes), please contact the publisher. Thank you for your support of the author's rights.

Yen On
150 West 30th Street, 19th Floor
New York, NY 10001

Visit us at yenpress.com
facebook.com/yenpress
twitter.com/yenpress
yenpress.tumblr.com
instagram.com/yenpress

First Yen On Edition: August 2022
Edited by Yen On Editorial: Jordan Blanco
Designed by Yen Press Design: Andy Swist

Yen On is an imprint of Yen Press, LLC.
The Yen On name and logo are trademarks of Yen Press, LLC.

The publisher is not responsible for websites (or their content) that are not owned by the publisher.

Library of Congress Cataloging-in-Publication Data
Names: Kennoji, author. | KWKM, illustrator. | Cash, Jan Mitsuko, translator.
Title: Hazure skill, the guild member with a worthless skill is actually a legendary assassin / Kennoji ; illustration by KWKM ; translation by Jan Mitsuko Cash.
Other titles: Hazure sukiru kage ga usui o motsu girudo shokuin ga jitsu wa densetsu no ansatsusha. English
Description: First Yen On edition. | New York : Yen On, 2021.
Identifiers: LCCN 2020055761 | ISBN 9781975318772 (v. 1 ; trade paperback) | ISBN 9781975318796 (v. 2 ; trade paperback) | ISBN 9781975318819 (v. 3 ; trade paperback) | ISBN 9781975347994 (v. 4 ; trade paperback)
Subjects: LCSH: Assassins—Fiction. | GSAFD: Fantasy.
Classification: LCC PL872.5.K46 H3913 2021 | DDC 895.63/6—dc23
LC record available at https://lccn.loc.gov/2020055761

ISBNs: 978-1-9753-4799-4 (paperback)
       978-1-9753-4800-7 (ebook)

10 9 8 7 6 5 4 3 2 1

LSC-C

Printed in the United States of America

HAZURE SKILL
THE GUILD MEMBER WITH A WORTHLESS SKILL IS ACTUALLY A LEGENDARY ASSASSIN

CONTENTS

1. Taking the Qualifying Exam 1
2. Assassination Commission 47
3. To the Duchy of Bardenhawk, Part I 69
4. To the Duchy of Bardenhawk, Part II 99
5. Starting with Collection Quests A to Z, Part I 131
6. Starting with Collection Quests A to Z, Part II 163
7. The Kidnapping Incident, Part I 175
8. The Kidnapping Incident, Part II 189
9. By the Manual 211
10. Princess Alias's Adventure Journal · 219

Afterword 231

1
Taking the Qualifying Exam

The branch manager, Iris, had called me into her office to talk.

"I think…this really won't do in the near future…," she told me.

"Do you think so?" I asked.

As usual, the office was bustling with adventurers who had made their way to our guild branch. One was going about routine business and detachedly accepting quests, another was complaining to an appraiser about their proof of quest completion or lack thereof, and a third was trying his luck with the female staff.

"This won't do…," Iris said, repeating her earlier remark while scowling. "No, this won't do at all…"

"Given your position as the branch manager, shouldn't you have the authority to do something about it?"

"If only. But that might create its own issues. Things like this, well, they need to be decided by the Adventurer Association—the big shots at headquarters. You never spoke a word of complaint, and I'd just turned a blind eye…"

"So you mean to say the situation has been exacerbated?"

"Yes."

The problem had begun when other branches requested that the guild master transfer me to their offices.

"Why haven't you complained about your salary?" Iris pressed.

"Because I wasn't dissatisfied with it," I replied.

"Of course *you* would say that... Still, you really should be making more."

Not long ago, Iris had been drunkenly begging me to stay. Did she want me to leave for more income or remain here?

"This took me by complete surprise...," Iris muttered, as she seemingly thought back to what had happened. "When the transfers were brought up, I was taken aback by the proposed salaries. I didn't think they paid so well. If you accept, you'll be making more than I do."

"Oh, really?"

"As indifferent as ever, I see. You could bother to act more astonished, you know."

"If the other branch managers are putting in offers for me, couldn't you do the same?" I suggested.

Looking apologetic, Iris answered, "We have set budgets for personnel expenses at each branch..." Then her voice dropped to a mumble. "I don't want another branch to take you from us, though..."

I didn't care, but evidently, Iris was set on giving me a raise. She was conflicted because she didn't have the power to grant it. I'd explained that I didn't require one, but she was intent on increasing my salary. Whether it was out of the kindness of her heart or because it weighed on her conscience, I couldn't say.

Iris hummed to herself, seeming rather busy with the predicament she herself had created—so much so, in fact, that her undergarments were on display for all to see.

"I don't intend to leave for another branch," I reassured her.

"But you only feel that way for the moment, right?"

I suppose she had a point. I guess she wanted confirmation I wouldn't change my mind down the road.

I placed my uniform jacket on Iris's lap.

"What's that for?" she asked.

"It's just… I can see your red panties," I replied.

"Yeep!" Iris let out a strange scream and quickly closed her legs. She glared at me with flushed cheeks. "…Pervert."

"You're one to talk, considering the risqué color."

"They're supposed to be *private*, as in, only I'm supposed to know…"

"Please rest assured that I won't go around telling others about them."

I'd once even removed her undergarments; it seemed such things embarrassed her.

"Oh. Maybe…"

Iris returned my jacket, then opened and rifled through her desk drawers. She pulled out a weighty stack of papers and began to search them for something.

"Just as I thought. This should solve the issue."

"What is it?"

"A license! That's the answer!" When I gave no indication I understood, Iris began to explain.

"Right now, Maurey and two others can act as appraisers, correct?"

"Yes. I believe Mr. Maurey has the Plant Master license, or something of the sort," I said.

"Exactly. Having a license is the equivalent of going out on quests yourself. Possessing one is grounds for a raise. This! This is it!" Iris clapped her hands together at the idea.

"The three appraisal licenses the guild grants are Plant Master, Item Scanner, and Enemy Expert...and what do you think happens when someone has all three?"

What *would* happen? I thought about it, but Iris continued before I could give an answer.

"If one collects them all, they'll be promoted to Lead Appraiser and get a raise!"

Apparently, there were other types of certifications, but those three were the main ones. The Plant Master license qualified an individual to appraise various flora, while the Item Scanner one was for magical objects, and the Enemy Expert one was for animals, monsters, and magical beasts. Each required a fair share of knowledge to acquire.

These qualifications were unnecessary for anyone with the Appraisal skill. I only knew of one individual in the capital who had that ability. However, Appraisal alone was enough to become a merchant, so anyone with it wouldn't go out of their way to work at a guild.

"If you think I should obtain those, then I'll do as you ask," I said.

"It's common for anyone aiming for a license to study for an entire year, but I suppose you wouldn't need to do that."

I was well aware people judged others by their qualifications and titles. If it would help me in the future, I saw no harm in getting certified now. It seemed I would need to travel to the guild headquarters in the capital to apply.

"For starters, why don't you get the Plant Master license? The exam should take two or three days. Including travel time, it should take one week."

Since I had Gate, I didn't actually need the extra time for the trip, but if Iris was giving it to me, then I would take it.

"All right. Then I'll come back next week."

"Okay. Do your best."

After Iris's words of support, I left the room and ran into Maurey.

"I heard what was up. You think you're gonna get the Plant Master certification?! You?!" I could practically hear the self-satisfaction dripping off his tone.

"We'll see. Can't know until I try," I replied.

"The written and the practical exams are both out of a hundred points, and I got a hundred ninety-two! Meaning I set the record for highest score. You think you can surpass me?!" Maurey prattled on feverishly, spittle flying out of his mouth.

...*I see.*

If I were to earn the Plant Master qualification, Maurey would no longer be the sole staff member with that certification. Evidently, he viewed me as a rival.

"Excuse me! What do you think you're doing yelling right in front of my door?" Iris emerged from her office, looking peeved. "Maurey, please keep your nose out of Roland's business and focus on your own work."

"...Yes, ma'am. I mean, the number-one guy in all of history has gotta be here to give some guidance to the rookie when he comes home after failing that exam."

Maurey was doing his best to be as patronizing as possible. He obviously expected me to fail, which only fueled my motivation to pass.

I said my good-byes and left the guild.

◆

When I told Rila about the matter, she decided to come with me.

"This should do it. Without a doubt!"

"*Heh-heh-heh.*" Rila laughed fearlessly as she stowed her coin purse, which was tied to a string. It was the second pouch I had bought her and was in the shape of a cat's head, just like the first.

"It cannot be pilfered, and I cannot drop it. It's brilliant, is it not?"

"Seems it is. I can see you're taking very good care of the present I got you."

"I-I am not, you fool. I am simply cherishing my money and making sure not to drop it or lose it. Do not grow conceited over this." Rila turned away from me.

Though many types frequented the capital, Rila's looks made her stand out. She had a certain dignity about her, perhaps because she had been the demon lord. There was a good chance she'd end up a target because she looked wealthy.

"You just need to be careful," I told her. "I'll go arrange to take the test for the license at headquarters."

"Mm-hmm. Well then, I shall have my fill of enjoying the markets."

We decided on our rendezvous point in advance, then parted ways.

Once I got to the guild headquarters, where the proctor training was held, I approached the counter and spoke to the staff. I told them my business, received a form, and filled it out.

"I've processed your information. The exams are each a hundred points and consist of a written portion and a practical that involves collecting the indicated plants. You can pass by scoring at least an eighty on each. Anything lower than that will mean you fail," an official explained.

This was basically in line with what Maurey had told me. The practical surely gave those who relied on book knowledge trouble. My dear senior colleague had once been a C-rank adventurer, so he must have done very well on that section.

The staffer informed me of the exam's date and time. There was an opening tomorrow, so I had the rest of the day to myself.

The registration process went much quicker than I'd expected. It was only just past noon.

Rila had been excited about walking around to grab a bite to eat, and there was still quite a bit of time until we were supposed to meet back up.

I walked around, weaving through the bustling marketplace, when I heard a loud and familiar voice.

"Stop right therrrrreee! Stoppp!"

Rila looked like she was on a mission as she sprinted through the crowd.

"...What is she even doing?" I said to myself.

I looked where she was headed. A little kid wearing a hood was nimbly darting between people, a certain cat-shaped pouch clutched in his hands.

"M-my purse!" Rila cried out, close to tears. "My precious purse! The one that Roland bought me!"

Apparently, she'd been pickpocketed, and the purse had been torn right off her string.

Some helpful citizens had tried helping upon seeing Rila's distress, but the thief evaded them as though he had eyes on the back of his head. He was quite agile. Perhaps he was relying on sound to dodge.

"Waaaaait! Waaait...pleeease..."

Rila was close to sobbing.

Still, I couldn't help but be impressed by how fast the pickpocket was. He'd make a fine assassin.

I sighed.

"Next time, I'll get her one with a chain."

The kid disappeared around a corner, purse still in hand.

I followed.

The kid glanced back at me. "Ahh! Another one?!" he exclaimed.

"Give back that purse. I know you stole it."

"Shuddup! Dummy!"

I ran a little faster, overtook the kid, and blocked his exit.

"Whaaa?! How'd you suddenly pop up right in front of me?!"

"Give it back. If you do, I'll only rough you up a little."

"What're you planning on doing to me, old man?"

Old man?

I'd expected the thief to stop in his tracks and turn around, but instead he scaled the alleyway wall up to the roof in no time.

"See ya!"

"Oh, interesting."

It seemed the kid wasn't just light-footed; he was acrobatic as well.

...Can't be human.

When the kid had leaped up, the force had blown off his hood to reveal two decidedly animal-like ears on top of his head.

"Must be a beastperson. Figures."

I found several footholds along the wall that I could grab on to. After quickly finding a path to the roof, I leaped and scaled the wall until I reached the top.

"Huh? Ahhh! He's climbing?!"

"Don't think you'll be able to run from me, kid."

"Th-this guy's not joking around..."

The color drained from the pickpocket's face as he hopped over

Chapter 1

to the next building. I pursued him and jumped from one roof to another.

"I'll give it back! I'll give it back!"

The kid tossed the purse as he fled. I picked it up only to realize it was empty.

"...So he only left it after taking the contents."

While I'd been checking for the cash, the little thief had snuck away. He apparently knew all the getaway routes in the capital, suggesting he did this regularly.

"Looks like it's time for some punishment."

The kid couldn't have gotten far. He was probably trying to lie low or put distance between us.

...There he is.

I spotted his ears, though only for a split second.

Now, I didn't use this trick often, but today I had little alternative. If I ran through the crowd, I wouldn't be able to catch up with the pickpocket. So, instead, I created my own footholds in midair using mana. They would disappear almost instantly, considering the limited mana I possessed, but a little was all I needed. I moved to the next platform before the previous one disappeared. After doing it a few more times, I'd gained some altitude.

The one drawback was that I couldn't stay in the same place for long.

The thief was concealing himself beneath overhangs, so I couldn't find him as easily from above. He looked around restlessly until he noticed me in the air.

"Uhahhhhh?! He's *flying* now?!"

"No, it may seem like I am, but I'm actually only temporarily solidifying the air using mana and jumping."

"I-I don't get it!" the kid exclaimed.

Thump, thump, thump. He started to run as I pursued him from the skies.

"Return the contents of the purse, beastperson."

"But there wasn't all that much in it! It was just five thousand rin! What's the big deal about losing that?"

"You cannot go around stealing from others. Didn't your mother teach you that?"

He shot me a glare in response. It seemed the beastperson even knew about the intricate alleyways. The boy didn't lose his way and swiftly headed forward without hitting any dead ends.

Ahead of him was the river that led out of the capital. That must have been his plan of escape.

"This is bad. This is bad. Who is that guy? He's messed everything up! How is he flying?"

The little pickpocket boarded a small boat tied up with a rope, pushed off the coast with an oar, and started to paddle. This, too, must have been something he regularly did, although he was now rowing for dear life. Once the current started to pull him along, he sailed rapidly downstream.

"Whew… Ha-ha-ha! See ya, old maaaan!"

Old man…

He laughed as he paddled, looking relieved. No doubt, he believed he'd gotten away at last. He stopped his noisy rowing and squinted over his shoulder.

Splash, splash, splash, splash.

"...? Is that the water...?" the kid said.

Liquid was easier to solidify than air.

"If I can walk through the sky, I'd obviously be able to walk on water."

"Stoppp iiiit! No mooore! Somebody help meee!"

"I've never allowed my prey to escape from me before. Not even once."

"Yeek?!"

The boy began to paddle as quickly as he could, but I was too fast for the boat.

I couldn't move at my usual speed because I had to make footholds using mana, but I was still fast enough. Once I reached the boat, the out-of-breath beastperson had given up.

"Fine, I'll give it back. I'll give it back already. Here, five thousand rin."

He rifled through his pocket and thrust some paper notes at me. I took them.

"You gave me a fair share of trouble," I remarked.

"I should be telling you that. You were after me like you were gonna kill me for barely any money... Who the heck are you, old man? That was ridiculous."

Old man...

"I'm a guild staffer from the Lahti branch."

"I-I didn't know they made guild workers like you. What's up with that? Have guild workers learned to fly recently?"

"Yes. They have."

"You liar!"

The beastperson child slumped as if to say, *Just do whatever you want with me.*

◆Roje◆

Meanwhile, at home…

"I expected this from the human, but to think Lord Rileyla would also be out again. Hrmm…" Roje hung her head, alone in Roland's house.

"Really now, where could they have gone?"

It had been three hours since Roje had stopped by, and there was no sign Rila or Roland would be back soon.

She glanced outside and noticed the sky had clouded over at some point. When Roje narrowed her eyes, she spotted white streaks falling from above.

"Rain? Oh, this is no good. I thought I saw their laundry outside!"

She rushed out through the back and carried a bundle of laundry back inside.

"…" As she returned to grab a second load, Roje suddenly stopped.

"These…these are Lord Rileyla's…panties… A-and they're incredibly scandalous… Th-the material is so thin in some spots… it's practically see-through!"

Even as the rain came down on her, Roje was too occupied with staring at Rila's undergarments to notice.

"..."

After checking her surroundings, Roje slowly unfurled the undergarment, forgetting that she was getting wet from the precipitation.

"A-as her follower, I must check whether they are comfortable to wear...especially since Lord Rileyla, our demon lord herself, must wear them against her bare skin..."

Huff, huff. Roje breathed heavily from her nose and thrust her leg through one hole of the panties...

"Oh my. Oh my, oh my, oh my, oh my, oh my... My, my, my, my, my!"

Roje timidly turned around and saw a flash of light—and the woman illuminated by it.

Dey wore her usual smile, but her eyes held a certain glitter to them, as though she had found a new plaything.

"D-did you see all of that...?!" Roje asked hesitantly.

◆Roland◆

After apprehending the pickpocketing beastperson in the capital, I brought him to Rila.

"Oh! My purse...! Did you retrieve it for me, knave?"

"I just happened to come across it."

"Of course you would! So...why the child?"

The young beastperson, who was cowering, eyed Rila with displeasure.

"Hey. Haven't you got something to say?" I said to him.

"I'm…sorry…"

Rila, who didn't seem especially upset, sighed and crouched to be at the kid's level. "Now that you have learned from this experience, you will never do it again, yes?"

"But…I don't have any money…," the beastperson child said, seeming close to tears.

"Mm-hmm…well, in that case…"

Rila opened her cat purse and took out a bill.

"Stop that, you dolt. That doesn't fix the problem."

Slums existed in the capital, just like any place, and children were no exception to poverty. Then again…this child had been trying to escape outside the capital.

"Where were you headed to in that boat?" I asked the kid.

"…Home… My mom…she's waiting for me."

"And what does your mother think of the money you've earned through stealing?"

"She…but…"

The kid's earlier vigor was nowhere to be seen. He whimpered and tears dribbled down his face. It didn't seem like a story we could talk about while standing in the street.

We headed into a restaurant to eat and talk.

The child ate like it was his first meal in a while. His name was apparently Jita.

"My mom is sick…and I need money to cure her."

Chapter 1   15

I glanced at Rila, but she shook her head.

"I do not know whether the same holds true for human healing magic... However, our type of magics generally increases an individual's natural recovery. It can be used to mend an external wound, but curing an illness is another matter."

The theory behind human and demonic healing magic was fundamentally the same.

"So you mean you're saving up for medicine then, Jita?"

"Yeah..."

Rila looked at me as though she were asking if anything could be done. But frankly, there wasn't.

Based on the situation, the mother was likely unable to work, and Jita's methods could hardly be dubbed commendable. They surely had nothing to eat if they couldn't earn a living.

"What of adventuring?" Rila asked me.

"It would take time. I would recommend it if he didn't have family, but..." I trailed off.

"One must cherish their family...," the demon lord finished, quite sappily.

I didn't really understand the emotions that came with having a family. Thinking back on it, there had been moments when I thought I might have come close, but my teacher and I weren't related by blood.

Based on what Jita had told us, the medicine cost about twenty thousand rin per week. A child couldn't earn that much through the proper channels.

"Could you not arrange a high-paying job for him?" Rila inquired.

"I could, but…while elves and beastpeople allied with humans during the war, there's still discrimination against them. I could find him good work, but his employer would likely exploit him."

"My, humans are so petty."

Rila was right. Nonhumans were often refused service at even slightly upscale restaurants.

Jita, who had been scarfing down food, stopped eating.

"Could I…bring this home? I want to share…with my mom…"

Tears welled up in Rila's eyes. Apparently, the idea that the demon lord was ruthless and cruel was a lie cooked up by humans.

"I'd like to talk to your mother," I told Jita. "Would you mind taking us to her?"

"Huh? To my place? …Sure."

Instead of having the child take home the leftovers, I ordered two more fresh dishes from the shopkeeper.

We left, and the three of us boarded the boat Jita had been attempting to escape in. We used it to leave the capital by way of a narrow irrigation ditch.

"There are troublesome guards if you head straight downstream," Jita explained.

We continued along until we reached a small dock by a water mill and stopped. Not too far away, there stood a lone building—Jita's home.

"I'm home," he called. When Jita came in through the door, a beastperson woman rose from the bed.

"Welcome back, Jita. Oh, and who are our visitors?"

"I ran into them, and they bought me food."

"Is that right? Thank you very much."

I handed over the meals from the eatery to Jita, and he headed into the kitchen with Rila where I could hear them chatting.

"Do you know how to cook?"

"Ha-ha-ha. Do not underestimate me."

They had really hit it off at some point.

I quickly introduced Rila and myself to the mother.

"I heard that you have been sick for quite a while..."

"Yes. I've caused my son nothing but hardship... I've told him so many times not to bother with the medicine..."

"You don't want it anymore? Why?"

"It can ease the symptoms, but it seems there's little hope for a cure..."

"...I see."

Rila and Jita were having fun in the kitchen.

Apparently, the mother had spoken with Jita about not taking the medicine, but he'd refused to listen and insisted she would get better.

"I have an inkling of what a beastperson child would need to do to make enough for my medicine. I want him to stop..."

I checked the note that the doctor had written for her. I didn't understand the treatment, but the medicine should have been a cheap purchase at any apothecary in the capital.

...Wait, but didn't she say it was incurable?

"What a frown. Come now, it's nothing you need concern yourself with, Mr. Roland."

The mother pointed at the wrinkles on my brow and laughed softly to herself.

Later, we ate the dinner Rila and Jita made, then rested.

"Roje may know of some herbs that could work," Rila offered. "She is one of the long-lived elves of the forests, after all."

"I'd say seven-tenths of her have rotted away, though."

"If there's anything she can offer, we should listen. We must jump home, knave. Roje may be there already."

"Understood."

◆Roje◆

"Commander Roje? What were you doing with Lord Rileyla's undergarments?"

"Uh. A-about those…"

Roje stood in the rain, thunder sounding overhead. Her eyes darted back and forth.

Dey was grinning cheerfully.

"I-I was simply helping Lord Rileyla with housework. Her clothes would have gotten wet if I had left them out, after all." Roje deftly hid Rila's panties behind her back.

"That wasn't what I was asking, though. Commander Roje, just now…you were wearing Lord Rileyla's undergarments."

"I-I was not! I was not!"

"Perverted elf. ♡"

"I'm nooot! Take it back! Take it back!"

"If Lord Rileyla were to find out, I wonder what she would say?" Dey giggled mischievously.

Roje the elf now seemed a mouse cornered by a cat. "Grrr... Y-you dare blackmail me...?! What do you want?!"

"Why, just to see the distress on your face, Commander Roje. ♡"

"You're even more twisted than I thought!"

"The magic division commander of the imperial guard... I wonder whether you would have wrapped her brazier around your head had I left you alone a little longer."

"Are you making a mockery of me, Candice Minelad?" Despite her biting words, Roje couldn't conceal how shaken she was after being discovered. "Who would ever sully my adored Lord Rileyla... and her panties in that way! What an unspeakable act!"

Dey's grin widened. "My, my. You're hardly one to talk."

At this rate, Roje would never live this down.

Gathering her remaining wits, the elf said, "Looks like I need to find a way to shut you up."

And her chosen method was brute force.

"I don't really care much since I'm dead...but you really are foolish if you expect to get away with threatening a vampire when it's practically evening..."

The sky had already grown dim. Roje had utterly forgotten the time.

It's already dusk? ...Wh-what do I do? I picked a fight with her... This is no good. I cannot fight a vampire in the darkness...

However, there was no going back now.

Roje thrust the panties into her pocket.

"I stake my honor upon it! I will silence you!"

Her chance at victory was slim, but fleeing would utterly ruin her reputation. She'd be Dey's plaything for the rest of her days. The only option was to try.

Roje cast her favored magic, Shadow Edge, on both of her hands. Two swords manifest in response.

Dey responded in kind. "Very well, I'll take you on. I've been feeling put out because Master Roland hasn't spent much time with me lately. I suppose you're as fair a distraction as any, Commander Roje. I feel so worked up at the thought of fighting a high-ranking member of the demon lord's army."

Dey summoned her bloodsucking spear.

"…"

"…"

Tension made the air heavy. They both moved at once. However, in the end, they did not exchange blows.

The owners of the mouse and the cat had come home.

"Stop that."

Roland had appeared out of nowhere, grabbing both women by their cheeks.

"Fmgh?!"

"Aww. No fair!"

"What do you think you are doing, you fools?" Rila scolded.

◆Roland◆

The next day, I took the written test for the Plant Master license in a room at the guild headquarters.

Chapter 1

There were two other men taking the exam with me. One was a spectacled guild worker. The other, to my left, was unshaven.

Iris had told me the test would be difficult, but I didn't have much trouble with it. I hadn't even had to pause once while going through it.

"*It's taboo to use knowledge or techniques of the woods, though…*" That's what Roje had said when I explained to her about Jita and his mother. "There is an herb called genosho. *It isn't very uncommon, but as far as the ways of the woods go, it's practically a cure-all… Well, I suppose I shouldn't go as far as to say that, but it's pretty close. It's worth a try.*"

Roje seemed so excited Rila had asked her for a favor that she happily told us all she could.

Apparently, the ways of the forest were only passed down among the elves. The rather isolated race was practically a group of recluses, so they likely knew of many things humans didn't.

I'd never seen Roje so enthusiastic before.

When I told her we would deliver the *genosho* once we found it, Roje claimed she needed to make some preparations and headed out with Dey.

"…"

I felt someone staring at me from the left. Actually, I had for a while now.

"Hey, lad, you got a sec?" the unshaven man, who seemed to be in his late thirties, asked. He was taking advantage of the fact that our proctor had fallen asleep.

"Would you let me have a look at your answers? Just even a

quick peek. Come on, kid, you look like you've got a good head on you."

"I don't think it means much if you cheat to succeed."

"Oh, c'mon, don't be so fastidious."

I didn't intend to continue with the argument, so I ignored him, which earned me a cluck of his tongue. The man didn't look like a guild worker. Having a license was a qualification all on its own, making it desirable for anyone in the health industry.

Though he hardly looks the part.

The proctor, who abruptly woke up, called time on the exam and collected the answer sheets.

To my right, the guild worker sighed and stood. "I thought this would be the year…but I guess I just can't do it. I'm giving up on the test…," he admitted before departing gloomily.

I'd taken a look at his answer sheet during collection. It had been half blank.

"Gutless," the unshaven man spat.

"Well then, it seems there are only two of you now. We'll move on to the practical. Please collect the herbs named on these forms by midday tomorrow and return here."

After that explanation, I glanced at the paper I had been handed. It listed roughly one hundred varieties of plants used as ingredients in medicine.

So I just have to collect these, then.

"Please be careful."

After the proctor left, the unshaven man glanced at my paper. "That's different from mine… Hey, lad, want to trade info?"

I didn't see how that would benefit me, as I already knew where to find everything.

"I know. I know. You're thinking we're not supposed to work together, yeah? But the proctor never said it wasn't allowed. You feel me?"

"I suppose you're right."

We had one day to collect a hundred varieties of plants on our own, but we'd be doing so unsupervised. It was very easy to cheat if you wanted to. Despite that, few still managed to pass the exam, suggesting some kind of trick.

Most of the herbs could be gathered close by, so the test wasn't demanding anything unreasonable.

"Lad, you used to do something pretty sketchy before, right? You haven't gotta say anything. I've got a good intuition for these things."

"If you were that insightful, you would've done better on the written portion."

"Don't give me sarcasm. This license is important to me. Think of it as an act of mercy…you got me?"

I'd feel remiss if I gave him concrete information. Instead, I told him he didn't need to go far for the collection and the herbs were all in season.

"I see… Who are you, lad? You know just about as much as the people making the exams."

"If you live in the woods as long as I have, you pick it all up naturally."

"Grew up feral, didja?"

If I headed to the nearest forest, I would be able to finish my task by nightfall.

When I set out from the capital, the unshaven man followed me to the plains. I picked the wildflowers and herbs from the list and put them into my jute bag.

Evidently, the man had some idea of what he was doing as well. He was also gathering his own herbs and talking at times, saying things like, "*Whoa, didn't expect to find this here.*"

"Despite appearances, I run an apothecary. I'm somewhat familiar with stuff, but there are these twenty species I just haven't got any idea about. I think each plant gathered probably counts as a point."

"Likely," I answered.

"If you don't have perfect knowledge of all this, you end up failing," he remarked.

"Is that right? But if that's the case, can't you take the test again?"

"I've got some money troubles, ya see. But things'd be different with a license. It kind of proves that you're reliable, that they can trust ya. At the guild, they only take herbs for regulation prices, but if you've got your own shop, ya get to set the price."

It seemed he planned on earning a larger profit by advertising that he was licensed.

"The only customer I've had lately is this useless brat, and my potions haven't been moving since the war ended. Well, it all goes to my liquor tab anyway."

I quietly listened to the unshaven man grumble to himself without letting on that I was eavesdropping.

As we headed deeper into the woods, he lamented his financial situation at every pause. This made it appear as though we were working together, but in actuality, the unshaven man had only decided to follow after me.

I ignored every question he tossed my way.

"Maurey received a high score, so I suppose he knew enough to pass the test."

"Didja say something?"

I shook my head.

Before long, I located some *genosho*, which had nothing to do with the exam, and plucked some of it.

"So, like I was saying, a shop really depends on regular customers." This guy sure knew how to talk about himself. However, there was something he said that caught my attention. "There's this beastperson kid who comes by once a month. I figure none of the other apothecaries will sell him anything. Ha-ha-ha. He just takes home the flour I give him, all grateful about it."

"..."

The man continued, as though he were telling a joke, "Who'd make actual medicine for a beastperson? Seems like the kid's got cash, though you wouldn't think it. He always pays up. Heh-heh-heh." He laughed unpleasantly and loudly.

I turned to face the unshaven man.

"That beastperson..."

"Hmm?"

"...Does he live outside the capital?"

"I think he mentioned something of the sort. I wouldn't be surprised if he was from the slums. The brat's filthy."

"What's his name?"

"...I think it was something like Jino? Jina maybe? Something like that."

Immediately, I grabbed the man's neck and pushed him against a large tree.

"Gah?!"

"I'll tell you what his name is... It's Jita. Do you have any idea how he's making that money he pays you with? Do you know why he needs that medicine?"

The man writhed in pain and scratched at my arm.

"Wh-what's wrong with you, lad? You know that brat or something? He couldn't have gotten the money through proper channels."

"That's right."

Next, I slammed him down onto the ground as hard as I could. He didn't even scream. Instead, he was twisting in silent agony.

"I'm amazed you actually are an apothecary."

"...Wh-what's your problem? What did I...ever do to you? I saw the medical note. That kid's mom will never get better."

"That's only true when it comes to human treatments."

"Look, all I did was sell the little brat hope—the possibility that his mom would survive!"

"Shut up, you fraud. If I know anything, it's that you weren't doing this with any good intentions."

Jita had been bringing this man money in exchange for useless flour...

"But he's a beastperson. Ha-ha-ha...why're you so worked up about him? I'm the one putting myself out there helping somebody who's not human. That's what *normal* people do."

Were beastpeople *normally* treated this terribly?

"Three years ago, on Pickel Hill in the former Duchy of Bardenhawk, one hundred thousand from the third division of the allied armies triumphed over the one hundred and thirty thousand from the demon lord's army. We forced through their front line, then used the momentum to crush the enemy... That's the picture everyone paints of it. But in reality, that victory was a trap meant to target our supplies."

This had happened long ago.

"By setting up a Gate, several demons launched a surprise attack on our center for provisions. All forces managing the area perished. Supplies that had been meant to sustain an army for a month went up in flames. The nearest unit didn't even notice. Instead, it was a beastperson far removed from the incident. They realized something was wrong using their sharp senses before anyone else. Thanks to them, we were able to limit the number of casualties. They saved one hundred thousand soldiers' lives."

We would have needed to temporarily withdraw had we been too late to extinguish the fire. The enemy's aim had likely been to pursue us during the retreat.

"Many people in the army saw beastpeople differently that day."

"Hmph. Bet that one didn't steal, though," the unshaven guy remarked, grinning. I grabbed his collar.

"You're the one making him do that!"

...I'd gotten emotional.

I needed to recenter myself, for I'd unintentionally let my animosity show.

The man's eyes went wide, and he foamed at the mouth. It seemed I'd really scared him. He'd even soiled himself.

I released his collar, tossing him away.

"Don't go near Jita ever again."

I didn't know how long the man was planning to stay on the ground, but we were in a forest. Hopefully, he'd get up before something happened, but unforeseen accidents were known to occur during the exam.

After quickly collecting the required plants, I used a Gate to jump home and gave Roje the *genosho*.

"Will this really cure her?"

"I'm not sure. However, it has a better chance than any human remedy."

Apparently, Roje could make quite a bit with the amount I'd brought her.

"I'll prepare it alone. No one look inside the room."

"I'm not interested in how you do it, so long as it gets made. How long do you think this amount will last?" I asked

"Around three months. Now, thank me, human. I am using a treasured elf method to make this for you," Roje replied.

"There's nothing more tiresome than a braggart. I'm heading back to the capital."

"W-wait! Listen to meeee!"

Dey giggled. "He just implied that you're tiresome, Commander Roje. He doesn't seem to care about your elf whatever-it-is in the slightest."

"Gah. You dare make a mockery of elves, you zombie vampire?"

"Oh my. That wasn't my intention at all. You're silly even to think that I care about the elvish ways in the first place."

Roje scowled and glared at Dey, who smiled and waved her off. There was no telling whether they got along or not.

"Anyway, Roje, you've been a real help," I said. "Thank you."

"...What's suddenly gotten into you? Lord Rileyla was the one who asked me to do this. Your gratitude is meaningless. Hmph," she snorted after berating me.

Before returning to the capital, I visited Iris at the Lahti branch and asked for her advice on a particular matter.

"Hmm. I see. That does sound intriguing."

It seemed she liked my suggestion.

"I'll need to talk to the neighboring branch managers, however." She paused for a moment. "Hey, will you be able to get to the capital in time? Aren't you in the middle of your test?"

"I'll be fine. Please don't worry about me," I assured her.

Once we'd finished our discussion, I finally jumped to the capital.

Rila had been wandering all around the city and had located a nice restaurant, so we ate there, then made for the inn. After enjoying ourselves in the bed, Rila rested her head on my arm as she told me, "I cannot promise that the mother will fully recover. However, Roje was confident it would be an improvement over the current situation."

She spoke in a whisper, but it was easy to hear in the quiet room.

"I must reward Roje in some way. Playing physician is far removed from her usual duties."

"She also told me she would check in with the military physician from the rebellion forces' base on the island. Roje is a very loyal follower," I replied.

"That she is—one to boast about."

That elf's blind loyalty was also her one flaw.

Rila traced her pointer finger over my chest. She followed my muscles, then caressed the scars on them.

"Humans are truly narrow-minded when it comes to appearances. I have heard that is the reason the elves withdrew into the forests. Once, they were more sociable."

People from all walks of life existed in the capital, but those outside the city were not accustomed to others and, thus, less welcoming. Although humans and demihumans had fought together during the war, it was unclear how many knew about it.

"...Have you been with an elf?" Rila asked abruptly.

"What are you talking about?"

"As I said… Have you shared a bed with an elf before…?" She looked straight into my eyes.

"I have," I replied.

"Hmph. Seeing as how they are perpetually young and *beautiful*, I'm sure that must have been a highlight for you during the Human-Fiend War."

Rila turned her back to me. She had said "beautiful" in a particularly pointed tone.

"Yes, it was."

"Guhhhhh...! At least make the slightest attempt to deny it. Do not compliment another woman in front of me."

"It wouldn't do anyone any good for me to lie."

"You've put me in a foul mood. I feel jealous..."

When I tried to pull away the arm Rila was resting on, she latched onto it tightly.

"...However will you lift my spirits?"

"Why are you asking me that?"

Rila peered up at my face. "All you must do is love me, and only me, for tonight." She wrapped her arms around my neck and pressed a kiss to my lips. "That is a privilege I shall only allow you to have, knave."

"It's quite a privilege indeed," I responded.

"In that case, shall we welcome daybreak pleasantly exhausted?"

"You mean you want to keep at this until morning?"

"Ha-ha-ha...it shouldn't be too much for you to handle."

Rila had been a young maiden just a moment ago, but her expression had turned carnal at some point.

◆

Slight fatigue hung over me as I headed to the guild headquarters after a simple breakfast on the inn's first floor. The night hadn't affected me much, even compared to days when I'd slept properly. Rila, however, was presently passed out in the room.

Roje stood in front of the headquarters.

"I heard you were taking your exam here," she explained. She thrust a small bag at me.

"You've already finished?" I asked.

"I had the army physician inspect it as well. She said even humans would have no trouble taking the medicine."

"Thank you. Rila said she would be rewarding you in some way."

"Really? That would be an honor."

There was something sticking out of Roje's pocket—a scrap of cloth.

It looked familiar... Was it Rila's underwear?

What's she doing walking around with that? I wondered.

I figured that maybe her silly loyalty had gone so far, now she wanted the panties of the target of her affection? Perhaps she had bought a pair of her own as a good luck charm. Whatever the answer, it felt a little uncouth. Had I accidentally glimpsed the dark inner workings of Roje's mind? Maybe she wanted it because it was one of Rila's personal effects and was therefore a quasireligious relic to Roje.

A relic...

I didn't get it.

"What? Do you still require something from me?"

"...No, nothing."

Roje tilted her head quizzically. Even Rila had likely yet to see this side of Roje. I'd need to warn her to be careful.

And to think, it was only yesterday that Rila had been praising the elf. Imagining how Rila would feel upon discovering this made me disappointed, too. I tried to be accepting of Roje, despite her shortcomings.

"Humans do have a bad habit of rejecting anything they don't understand," I remarked.

"……? Yes, I suppose you're right about that," Roje replied.

I pocketed the medicine and entered the guild headquarters. When I went to the reception window, I found the same receptionist from the day before going through documents.

"Um, excuse me. About the Plant Master practical exam from yesterday…"

"Oh, yes, of course. Did you have a question? You have until this afternoon, so please don't lose hope and do your best."

"I'm done."

"What? That was quick." The staffer couldn't conceal her surprise. "We've only had ten others in the past who finished the exam so quickly. Two of them were desperate to pass, and the other eight had gotten help and ended up losing points because of it."

"You can tell they had assistance?"

"Yes. We don't tell the examinees, but we do a final quiz on the collected plants."

Of course. That was how they determined who'd cheated.

A person could get outside help collecting herbs, but they'd still need time to memorize information on the plants, and one day wouldn't be enough. While an applicant could complete the practical section swifter with help from others in the city, they still wouldn't pass without adequate knowledge.

I handed over the herbs I'd picked and my list to the receptionist. Then I was taken to the same room as yesterday.

"…Well then, I will start."

"Please," I said.

The final quiz was on all hundred varieties.

I was questioned on many fine details, starting with fundamentals, such as where each plant grew, the necessary germination conditions, when they would flower, and their potency. There were even some queries only an enthusiast would know.

"...Uh, guh...what...? You mean you didn't cheat...?"

"I didn't," I replied.

"But this *tochuso* here is supposed to only grow in very dangerous places and should have taken a lot of time to gather."

One should never underestimate a former assassin. I couldn't say as much aloud, of course.

"This is one nasty test. I can't believe you would make anyone go all the way there to harvest plants."

"But...this exam is designed for people to fail...!"

I'd felt the questions I'd been asked were rather spiteful, but they hardly fazed me. So I decided to fire back a spiteful inquiry of my own.

"*Tochuso* grows in places with a high elevation and good sunlight."

"So? What about it?"

"There's another kind of spot where it grows even better. Do you know where that might be?"

"...Huh?" My proctor couldn't answer. He gave me a severe look, then let out a laugh as though admitting defeat. "Mr. Roland, you scored perfectly on the written and practical portions. So perfect, in fact, that I'd suspected you of cheating... I must apologize."

The proctor bowed his head.

"I think it actually would have been more difficult for me to get answers wrong."

"Ha-ha...well, now you've said it. You've gotten the highest score in our history and at record speed, too. Congratulations. You've earned the Plant Master license."

"Thank you."

Apparently, I would be receiving a badge they would send to my local guild later. It must have been the one that Maurey proudly showed off while hitting on women.

"Did you used to be an adventurer?" the proctor asked me. "Or perhaps the apprentice of an apothecary?"

"No, neither. I was an assassin."

The proctor laughed at my response. "You're quite the knowledgeable assassin then. I suppose your specialty was poison?"

"Depending on the situation, I did have to make use of some."

It was the truth, but I don't think he believed me.

"What an interesting person you are," the proctor commented with a smile before leaving the room.

With the Plant Master qualifying exam complete, I went to the inn to wake Rila so that we could eat lunch.

"Ngh...still...sleepy..."

"This only happened because you got so caught up in the moment and wanted to keep going until morning."

Rila rubbed her eyes as she sipped her soup. She was spilling it a little.

"I got the medicine from Roje. We're taking it over to Jita."

"Mm-hmm… How are you so perky?"

"Perky in which way?"

"In both ways."

"I trained so I would be."

"In both ways?"

"In both ways."

"My…what lecherous training that must have been…"

By the end of the meal, Rila's drowsiness was gone, and she was ready to leave the city for Jita's house.

I didn't know whether to mention what had occurred with Roje, but with how much Rila had praised the elf, I found it a difficult subject to broach. Perhaps I'd gotten the wrong idea from the scant strip of cloth I'd seen. Maybe Roje had bought the undergarment for herself.

"Do you believe Jita's mother will get better?" Rila asked.

"I'm not sure," I replied.

"What an insensitive man you are. Can't you at least say something to give me peace of mind?"

"If doing so would increase the chances of her being cured, I would."

If Iris was able to get through to the others, Jita would have a means of income. There was nothing more I could do about that situation besides pray.

No sooner had we arrived at Jita's home than he came outside to meet us.

"Oh, welcome. What happened?"

"We have medicine for your mom."

"Huh? For my mom?"

Once I nodded, Rila bent down to meet Jita's eyes. "It's a secret medicine made by an elf. I am sure it shall make your mother feel better." She grinned.

"Th-thank you!"

A secret medicine? Roje hadn't called it that.

"Rila, don't raise his hopes. That won't do any good. You need to tell him the truth."

"How foolish. Stop your fussing! It is worse to make him feel anxious! Really now, a cold-blooded mortal such as yourself has no understanding of others' feelings."

When a demon was the one telling you as much, you didn't have any ground to stand on.

Jita's eyes went wide as though he'd remembered something.

"Oh, but... I don't have any money..."

"That won't be necessary. We didn't bring this to sell it to you," I explained.

Jita's eyes seemed to ask Rila and me if that was all right. We both nodded together.

"Jita, do we have visitors?" Jita's mother called from inside.

"Oh, yes. Roland and Rila."

"All right. I'll explain how this medicine works," I said.

"You will not. Allow me," Rila corrected.

She pushed me aside and entered the house, making her way to the bed in the back.

Since the two of us were now alone at the door, I decided to raise the matter I'd been thinking on.

"Jita, how would you feel about working at the Adventurers Guild?"

"Huh? At the guild?"

The boy's eyes went wide as I explained it to him.

"Do you know Lahti? It's slightly to the southwest of here. It's your average town." He nodded, so I kept going. "There's a lot of new adventurers near there. Rookies need to go to the mountains and forests more often, because there are a lot of different types of easy quests in those regions. However, beginners tend to overestimate their abilities, so a surprising number of them get lost and can't find their way home."

"Wooow...that seems silly of them."

"Come now, don't say that."

F-rank adventurers were the most likely to not report back for over a month after accepting a quest.

Quests that required battle only started at E rank, and we wouldn't send adventurers at that level to dangerous areas, either. The guild believed that most of the people who broke contact had been the victims of accidents. Rookies didn't understand the realities of adventuring and were more likely to get reckless, after all.

Inside, Rila was doing her best to explain things using gestures.

"I'd like you to guide lower-ranking adventurers," I said.

Jita pointed to himself. "...Me?"

"Yes. Your sight, smell, and hearing exceed the average human's. This work is ideal for you."

"I guess so...but you think I could really do it...?"

"It's not a question of whether you can or can't. I'm asking whether you will or won't."

He could become an adventurer himself, but that could wait until later.

"I'll do it. I'll take the job."

"Hmm. Good answer."

I gave him an approving pat on the head, which Jita responded to by squinting happily.

Now that I'd finished my discussion with him, I prepared to tell his mother about it. She seemed worried, but was happy Jita was so motivated.

"We're beastpeople. I'm not sure whether we can get proper jobs. Mr. Roland, I leave my boy in your hands."

"You can count on me."

"Thank you for everything, truly."

Jita's mother bobbed her head, which prompted Jita to do the same.

"Thank you…very much."

"No. We're not even sure if this will cure—"

Rila punched me in the back. I looked over, and she was rather furious and shaking her head. Evidently, she didn't want me volunteering any unnecessary information.

It seemed Rila had already gone over everything relevant about the medicine, and Roje had included directions in the bag on how to take it.

"How can we possibly thank you?" the mother wondered.

"It'll be a great help to us to have Jita around. That's enough," I assured her.

After that, we spoke for a while, then left Jita's house.

We headed back to Lahti, and I went to the guild to report on my test result.

"Oh, Mr. Rolaaand. How did the exam go? Have you finished already?" Milia was the first to spot and greet me.

"Yes. I passed it without incident."

"Wooow! Of course you did, Mr. Roland. We really ought to celebrate."

Hoping to dismiss that notion, I began to say, "It's not that big of a deal, so—"

"There's your humility again. It's a *very* big deal! So we all need to commemorate it."

Because Milia was speaking so loudly, everyone in the office had heard.

"Congrats, Argan! Did you study?"

"What? You didn't? Most people...spend years preparing."

"Mr. Argan, well done!"

"Congratulations!"

Everyone was talking to me, which made me feel somewhat embarrassed.

Maurey was apparently out for the day. He would've only caused trouble, so I was glad he wasn't around. When I went to the branch manager's office, I wasn't even given the opportunity to say how I'd performed. Iris had already heard it all.

"Milia is so loud. I knew you'd be fine, but I'm still thankful you made the cut."

"Thank you. So about the matter of the guide?"

"I asked three branches, and all of them okayed it."

Iris and I discussed the new guide system for a short while.

We would have permanent supporter guides on certain days of the week for the towns and three forests where most low-level quests took place. When guild staffers arranged quests, they'd also recommend that any F rankers traveling to a location for the first time go on days when a guide was available.

"...Well, I suppose this will do," Iris said.

"The woods aren't deep, but rookies get lost on unfamiliar paths because they let their guards down," I responded.

Many say carelessness is one's biggest foe.

Iris sighed in exasperation, then propped her head on her hand and smiled.

"You really are such a softie."

"...Am I?"

"You didn't know?"

"I simply thought of an effective system and found an appropriate person to fill the role at the opportune time."

"We'll leave it at that, then," Iris said. Then she laughed.

◆

A short time later, the new guide program's inaugural day arrived.

"I'm so nervous..." Jita had been preparing, talking to adventurers, and doing some easy wayfinding for others. Evidently, even that still left him unsure. "But I'm gonna work hard! Thanks to the medicine, Mom's been doing better."

"I'm glad to hear it."

About two months later, Jita's mother was cured before she had even finished using all of the medicine.

It seemed that Rila hadn't been wrong to boast about the efficacy of secret elf techniques.

Jita had said he wanted to thank us, so Rila, Roje, and I decided to have a meal together at Jita's house to celebrate his mother's recovery.

"Jita's been getting good reviews at his job."

"Oh, has he?"

Jita laughed with embarrassment at that.

The new system had been favorably received. Enough so that there were talks about recruiting more guides. New adventurers were very grateful to have someone supporting them, and this kept them from getting lost around forests and villages.

"They really underestimate the woods. There was even somebody who said today was his first time. I told him it was dangerous, but as soon as I looked the other way, he was wandering off on his own, and then—" Jita was complaining, but he was clearly grateful regardless.

Compared to when he had stolen Rila's purse, he looked a lot more cheerful.

"I'm going to treat you to a meal sometime with my salary, Roland!" Jita proclaimed.

"Sure, but it'll cost you."

"What? Go easy on me…"

"I'm kidding."

"It sure is hard to tell."

The three women in the room laughed.

Rila and Roje serenely watched the mother and son talk to each other. The pair looked nearly saintlike, although I had an inkling that they were pleased about slightly different things.

2
Assassination Commission

We were deep in the forest on an unnamed mountain in the northeastern part of the Felind Kingdom.

"*Wheeze, wheeze, haah...* Knave...do we have much farther to walk?"

"Yes. You're getting your just desserts for not exercising. We've hardly done anything yet."

"Hey, human, do not mock Lord Rileyla!"

"Shut up, you perverted elf."

"Grrr..."

Behind me was Rila, who seemed dog-tired as she walked, and Roje, who was practically glued to her.

The Rila's panties incident... That's what I was calling it now. I could have revealed it, but I'd chosen to wait for a while, biding my time until the moment was right.

Rila did her best to keep up with me, huffing and puffing as she did.

We'd crossed the most difficult part of the peak and were trekking through the woods. This was difficult for Rila, as she currently had the stamina of an average person.

"Really now, what an absolute pity... I had been in a picnicking mood, too..."

"I told you several times we weren't going on any picnic."

"Lord Rileyla is exhausted. I request a break to eat!"

"Only because you're hungry, I'm sure," I replied.

Walking the rough trail, which hardly constituted a real path, demanded more energy than I had accounted for. The trees all looked the same, an anxiety-inducing sight if you were unaccustomed to them. It could wear on the mind.

It had all started when I'd gone drinking last evening with Rila.

"*I...live with you, knave...yet I know nothing about you...,*" she'd said. I remembered the heartbreak in her misty eyes, though that might have been the alcohol. She'd slumped onto me as I sat on the sofa, then wrapped her arms around me. After taking a sip of her wine, she shared it with me through her own lips. I was hardly inebriated, but the drink helped the words flow.

"Do you want to see it, then? I'm not sure if it's still there, though." I'd been referring to the house in the mountains where I'd grown up. Rila nodded enthusiastically. Come the next morning, I regretted letting that slip, but there was nothing to be done about it by then.

I did my best to give Rila noncommittal replies, but she was intent on seeing my old home. And that's what led to us setting out along this northeastern mountain pass at daybreak.

The absurdly loyal elf who'd tagged along hadn't been part of the plan, but she happily watched over Rila for me, so I was glad to have her. Rila had packed food, a picnic blanket, hats, and canteens yesterday, but the extra baggage was little more than a nuisance.

Reaching the capital from my childhood home took the average person a day to get through the mountains and then another four on horseback. I hadn't known that when my teacher had told me, "*It takes two days to get to the capital—just two. It's not that far away.*" So I'd been convinced that was normal and did just as she'd said.

When I first went to the capital on my own, I'd taken four days for the round trip, and she hit me. That was when I realized my teacher had meant two days total for the entire journey.

I hadn't walked these woods in a long time, yet they hadn't changed in the slightest. They had been my training and hunting grounds and had instructed me in the ways of nature.

"Slow down," Roje called. "Have you no consideration for Lord Rileyla?"

"If you don't like my pace, you can turn around and go home."

"Why you little... Know your place, human!"

Rila didn't like it when I was considerate of her—at least not in this way. Apparently, it made her feel like she was holding me back.

Regardless, how she felt and reality were separate matters. Since Roje's nagging was also beginning to get on my nerves, we took a quick break, then resumed the hike.

After many brief stops along the way, we finally arrived at our destination sometime after noon. The copse of trees gave way to an open meadow of tall weeds and an old house overtaken by ivy that had even swallowed the door.

I'd thought thieves might try to take up residence here, but the place seemed abandoned.

"Is this it?" Rila inquired.

Nodding, I answered, "Yes."

"Oh-ho." She took a keen interest in the old building, walking a loop around it before returning back to me.

Meanwhile, Roje investigated our surroundings, muttering, "There's nothing here. What a lonely place."

"It feels entirely different from the elvish woods, doesn't it?" I offered.

"The forest I am from is... Well, it does not matter. Let us go inside for the time being."

"Sure," I replied.

Despite being only just after midday, the woods could get dark quickly. It was best for us to set up camp before nightfall.

I pushed aside the vines and headed inside.

How many years had passed since I'd been here? My life here had ended at the age of fifteen, when she had decided I'd come of age. After that, I'd taken up a secret life, traveling from region to region and moving from one country to the next as I fulfilled assignments. I'd used this place as a safe house several times, but only for a week at a time at most.

"*Cough, cough.* It's rather dusty. Roje, the window, if you would."

"As you wish. HRAAGH!" Roje energetically threw open all the windows one after another with impractical vigor. "I, Roje Sandsong, shall do all in my power to ensure Lord Rileyla has a comfortable stay. I shall clear this dust away as if my life depends on it!"

It seemed Roje was quite excited to spend some time with Rila away from home. She was more enthusiastic than usual.

This place was roughly the size of my present house, complete with three bedrooms, a living room, a kitchen, a dining room, a toilet, and a bath.

"Hmm. So you spent your days, morning to night, training in this place since you were an urchin, knave?"

Rila sat on the sofa and looked out the windows Roje had just opened. There was nothing but weeds there now, but it was where I'd been taught how to assassinate, fight, and use weapons.

"It wasn't just me. My teacher also grew up here."

"...And I'm sure your teacher was a woman," Rila commented.

"Yes. I'm surprised you guessed that."

"I just assumed she would be that which I did not desire." Rila snorted, a delicate expression on her face.

I brought several bits of wood over and used a thin knife to whittle away at them to start a fire. Once it grew large enough, I fed the logs to the flames.

"What is it you want to know about me?" I asked.

Coming here wouldn't reveal much to Rila on its own. It would've been far less work if she'd just asked directly.

"I simply wished to view the world as you have seen it."

"When did you become a poet?"

"S-stop that."

I never enjoyed discussing my past. Over the years, I'd consciously erased a lot from my memory.

"I am the daughter of the former demon lord, and I was once a magical prodigy. In some ways, my upbringing may have been similar to that waif's, Almelia."

I could easily imagine that. Hell and the human lands were different, but Rila and Almelia were both the offspring of kings. Rila was undoubtedly curious because my life as a social outcast was so different.

"You may tell me anything. I would like to know how you lived and what led us to meet. That is all I desire."

Tongues of flame peeked from between the gaps of the thick firewood.

"...When I was younger, I would often watch over the fire like this. My teacher was like a parent to me. She raised me and gave birth to the assassin I am. While she cooked, I would watch the stove and feed the flames. I used to poke the fire with an iron. I'm sure that having me hanging about was a nuisance while she cooked."

Rila laughed quietly behind me. "So there was a time when you were cute."

I heard the sound of something pop as Rila pulled a cork from a bottle of wine. She poured it into a glass she produced from her bag and tipped it back, quickly draining the contents.

"That's the reason your bags were so heavy," I stated.

"Yes, yes. I'm very stubborn," Rila quipped. Then she started to share some stories about herself. "By the time I was five, I could easily use court-order-rank tri magic. I'm sure I had my limitations, but I could cast the spells I taught you—Dispell and Shadow—without much trouble."

"And Roje?" I pressed.

"Roje would have only been capable of court-order-rank penta magic. I believe only half of the senior officers by my father's side could use court-order-rank tri magic. I attempted Raise, the forbidden necromancy spell, when I was nine. My father was so furious that I believed he was going to kill me." Rila chuckled as she recounted the incident. She'd told me about resurrecting her dead cat in the past.

I supposed it was my turn.

"...We'd receive letters for commissions from that opening there."

There was no delivery tray for the slot, so when mail arrived, it rustled as it dropped to the ground.

"When I heard the mail arrive, I picked it up and brought it to my teacher. There were several ways we received requests. When sent as letters, they changed hands several times. The deliverer and the person who'd handed them the letter never knew the original sender. However, they still understood enough to realize that opening the envelope endangered their lives. Each time the mail came, my teacher left home for a while. Sometimes it was a few days. Other times it was weeks. I always did as she instructed while on my own, training hard in the fields and the woods."

Rila slowly stood, her glass still in hand.

"Hmm? Is that one of the letters you mean?"

"What?"

"The envelope is nearly the same color as the floor, so perhaps we missed it coming in, yet...it looks recent." Rila picked up the envelope and handed it to me.

"..."

Chapter 2 53

"Will you not read it?"

"I don't do that type of work anymore."

When I tried to toss it into the stove's flames, Rila took it from me.

"In that case, I shall inspect it. It should not matter, since you intend to toss it away."

"Do as you like."

Rila tugged on the wax seal and tore the letter open, then pulled out the piece of paper and read it. "Hmm. Amy... Is that your teacher?"

"Yes. Wait, it's addressed to Amy?"

"That is the name written here, yes."

Just as I used the name "Roland" with people I trusted, *she* often used "Amy" with those close to her. Actually, it was the opposite. She had taught me to use false names to make jobs easier.

I wondered if she'd used this place as a safe house as I had. That, or the client hadn't known where to find her and sent it here.

"I was convinced it was for me."

"There are some parts I cannot read."

"That's not surprising." I took the paper and held it to the stove, which revealed the writing. "We can read it like this."

"Oh-ho. A trick!"

I handed the letter back to Rila, and she read through it again.

"An assassination commission...," she murmured.

"Of course."

"No...of an assassin. It's a request to kill an assassin."

"To Amy? Why?" I asked doubtfully, to which Rila responded

by handing the letter to me. The neat handwriting stated exactly what Rila had told me.

I am sure you have heard by now news of the Moisandle family's downfall as well as that of the Cuthra family that reigned over the port town to the west. There are rumors among the aristocrats that His Majesty has a secret agent raised from birth as a spy who collects information and dispatches assassins as the need arises. Although it was overshadowed by the Moisandles' downfall, a captain of the Order of Chivalry was supposedly murdered in the streets of Imil. Do you know anything of it, Amy? I have a hefty purse to offer. I would like you to investigate and, should you find the culprit, I would like you to take care of the matter.

Hmm. *I see,* I thought.

It seemed that aristocrats had assumed the "special public welfare division" lie that I'd adopted on a whim as a cover story was a genuine royal initiative. Though the two noble houses had indeed fallen, the two nobles themselves were still alive. They had likely been the sources of this misinformation.

"Knave, you have no lack of fans, I see."

"I did take down that underground arena, after all."

The nefarious aristocrats saw a larger conspiracy at work, but it had all been my doing. Still, it wasn't illogical for them to assume a royal order had been issued, even if their ire was off the mark.

Rila narrowed her eyes. "This all seems innocuous now, but there may be some extremists among this outraged group..." It was a deduction worthy of the former ruler of all demons. She possessed good intuition.

Chapter 2   55

"Almelia is at the castle," I said, suddenly feeling anxious.

Almelia... I still thought of her as that little girl on the battlefield. She didn't seem ready to hold her own to me.

"Mm-hmm...Almelia could be targeted. I doubt there are any as capable as you, however, so she should be fine."

We still couldn't discount the possibility of a coup d'état, though...

Because King Randolf had recently been punishing nobles publicly, other members of the aristocracy had to be cowering at the idea they might be next. I supposed anxiety and nerves could hasten them toward paranoia. I'd have to inform King Randolf about this letter soon.

The sender had naturally concealed their identity. I could tell special techniques had been used on the message, but I couldn't figure out what they were. If the client knew about the name Amy, they had to be someone she trusted.

She had likely shared some sort of key with the client that only the two of them could use—likely a manaprint, which could identify a person like fingerprints. Since that required using one's own magical power, only my teacher could determine the sender.

"I can't tell who they are, but the client must have assumed they would be assassinated, so they're definitely involved in something nefarious."

"Here I thought the war was over, yet humans still squabble amongst themselves... The human aristocracy is full of idiots."

Roje was fast at work, cleaning at the end of the hallway. I could hear the sound of her movements clearly even from the quiet living room.

Rila snickered. "So you have learned of information you would never have expected, it seems."

"Someone who believes they will be assassinated hiring their own assassin as a guard stands to reason," I replied.

"Is this what they mean by the saying 'fight fire with fire'?"

"Well," I said, "until I know who the sender is, I won't be able to assassinate them anyway."

I headed to the kitchen to cook our meal.

We had all the utensils needed, so I began to prepare the plants we had gathered on the mountains on the way here and the horned rabbit we had captured.

"You are cooking tonight, knave?"

"It's something I used to eat back in the day. Don't expect it to taste good, though. Did you enjoy your picnic?"

"I am exhausted, but I am glad to have learned something about you I did not know. It seems you truly are human. It's reassuring to learn that."

"What else could you have possibly thought I was?"

Rila propped her head on her hand at the table Roje had cleaned. She stared at me with a smile on her face.

"I am sure this lifestyle of yours must have been enjoyable."

"Perhaps it was."

Still, I had no plans to quit my work at the guild. As I had that thought, far more faces surfaced in my mind than before. There was Milia, Iris, and all of the adventurers. I was surprisingly happy to think they relied on me for things other than assassination.

Roje finally returned from her cleaning.

"You bastard...you're collecting points with Lord Rileyla by cooking?! You underhanded scoundrel!"

I didn't understand what she was going on about, but it seemed she didn't appreciate that I was in charge of tonight's meal. We placed the wine and bread that Rila had brought on the table, as well as the dinner I made.

My salt-broiled monster meat was well received.

"The fattiness and the seasoning are excellent, and the sautéed wild plants you used as a garnish are in perfect combination. By eating the vegetables between each bite of meat, the heartiness of the fat is tempered and makes it all taste more delicious." Rila complimented my work at length.

"Damn it. It's delicious..." Roje looked conflicted as she devoured the food.

Once we were finished, we turned in early because of how exhausting the journey had been. We'd decided to each take one of the bedrooms, but Rila snuck into mine. We talked to each other about what Roje might say in the morning for a bit, but Rila quickly passed out.

I listened to her gentle breathing as I stared at the ceiling. Coming here had brought back memories I could do without...

"This isn't what I'd planned."

It happened the year I turned fifteen. My teacher had acknowledged I'd grown into my own, though I still didn't know why she'd suddenly decided that. I was no match for her, and I hadn't completed any difficult jobs yet, either.

"*You've turned out to be a surprisingly good assassin.*" She had patted my cheek and grinned. *"If you keep up the hard work and stay ambitious, I'm sure you'll become a man capable of defeating me in another decade."*

"...I'm sure I'll be dead by then. Even if I were alive, I couldn't imagine beating you."

"Ah-ha. You feel that way now, but if you don't, I won't know what to do with myself."

"...Why's that?"

"Because it's my dream."

"What?"

At some point, I'd grown taller than her. I could dodge when she tried to hit me after I made mistakes. When she hugged me, I no longer ended up buried in her chest.

She had hugged me and stroked my back, perhaps as a way of saying good-bye.

"If I'm by your side, you won't grow. If you keep learning from me, you'll just become a lesser version of the assassin I am."

"...You're probably right."

"Same lack of charm, I see. Ha-ha. You don't need to become something else. Just dive deeper. Grow into yourself."

I hadn't understood her meaning at the time, but those were the last words she spoke to me. After a peck on my cheek, she'd disappeared. Or maybe I just hadn't been capable of seeing her leave.

It never occurred to me I might live another decade after that.

◆

Chapter 2

After reading the letter, King Randolf said, without the slightest surprise in his voice, "Well, I was expecting a few of them to start hating me. Really now. All I did was give them their just desserts for their crimes. This is why no one likes aristocrats…" He sighed, clearly frustrated. "If this other assassin is as good as you, there'd be no point in defending myself, but I will pray that they are a foe I can cope with and shall take the necessary countermeasures."

"I hope your preparations hold against the one you're up against," I replied.

"Well, you've sure gotten sentimental."

"I meant that as one of your close friends."

King Randolph grinned. "…You really have changed, Roland."

Once Rila, Roje, and I had exited the woods, I'd split off from them. Those two were likely plodding toward Lahti right now.

"This may be unnecessary, but…" I handed the king a note I had written the night before.

"What's this?"

"It's an assassin's usual methods of operation. The details are by no means infallible, but it's better to know than to not."

"Oh-ho. Hmm… It seems your *normal* way of life has taught you how to be kind."

"Don't mock me," I said, which made King Randolf laugh.

With nothing left to discuss, I started to leave, but the king stopped me. "Roland, how much does the Adventurers Guild know about you?"

"Why are you suddenly asking me that?"

"Lady Leyte of the Duchy of Bardenhawk has recently taken an interest in the organization."

Apparently, this matter had come up when she visited my house.

"You mean Maylee's mother…? What's the issue?"

"Before the Human-Fiend War, Bardenhawk didn't have a guild system, but now she's planning to adopt one. However, she has no one to manage the operation or to tell her what an adventurer should be. She's requested to borrow a strapping fellow who can help. What do you say, Roland?"

"I'll warn you that while I'm very good at making a system more efficient, I'm not suited for building something from scratch."

"You wouldn't be alone. I'd like to send out people to train the staff and some adventurers to act as examples as well," King Randolph said. According to him, Tallow, who had been present when Lady Leyte had raised this idea, had already approved of it. "I think Tallow will call upon you sometime later, but you're already here, so I thought I might as well tell you. We talked about who we'd send, and you were the first person to come to mind. Tallow agreed."

"It seems Mr. Argan the guild worker has earned a fair share of your trust."

"Come now, don't be so sarcastic. We might select the people who go, but there's also a possibility we'll just leave the matter to you."

"I do have the right to refuse, don't I?"

A strained look flashed across King Randolf's face. "Er, well…

Chapter 2

I suppose so, but...you have your own connections with the duchy, right? I was really hoping you'd lend a helping hand..."

"So if I were to go to Bardenhawk, what then?"

"Hmm?! Oh yes! What is it you'd like?" King Randolph had assumed I'd refuse the offer, so when I showed the slightest interest, he swiftly latched on.

"It doesn't have to be all of them, but I'd like to bring just a few specific people with me. That includes adventurers and guild workers."

"Mm-hmm. I will inform Tallow."

"This is all hypothetical, of course—just a possibility," I reminded him.

King Randolf looked dissatisfied with that. *"Don't give me that"* was written all over his face.

"...I'd like to talk to someone first. I'll give you my answer based on how that conversation goes... What are you grinning for?"

"To think you were once a cold-blooded assassin, and now you need to discuss your plans with someone... Heh, it's a woman, right?" King Randolf remarked.

"Think what you like."

"Oh, don't be so coy."

He poked me. The moment his finger met the palm of my hand, I pushed him away.

"Yee-ouch! You've sprained my finger!"

"Don't make such a big deal over a simple injury."

"...I can't believe you would harm a king's digit..."

"If you want me to treat you like a ruler, then I will next time."

King Randolf blew on his finger. "...No, it's fine. Just be your usual self, please."

"What's your actual aim with sending out guild workers?" I questioned. "You're not the type to do philanthropic work."

"I am currying favor while I can. I want everyone to think of us as a friendly country, both domestically and internationally. Something like that anyway."

"I thought as much. You've got a dark side."

"And the greatest reason of all is because Lady Leyte is a looker!" the king admitted with a laugh.

What a shrewd old man. After that, we talked for a while longer, and then I left.

"That is what you spoke of?"

When I explained my meeting with King Randolph to Rila, her eyes widened in surprise.

She and Roje were already home by the time I returned. At the moment, we were eating dinner, courtesy of Roje. It wasn't bad, but it also didn't taste particularly great.

"How is it, human? Now you see what I am capable of!" Roje, wearing an apron and holding a ladle, laughed while looking down upon me smugly.

It seemed she felt a need to prove herself because my cooking had been well received. She snuck occasional glances at Rila, hoping for commendation, but the former demon lord was occupied with other matters.

Chapter 2

"Hmm. I see," she said, completely ignoring Roje. "Maylee's country…"

"If you have any objections, I could travel through the Gate alone."

"No, that is not what I am concerned about. What do you think of it, knave?"

"It would be interesting work, though it would take a lot of effort. Plus, Maylee was the first person I taught my techniques. I'd be lying if I said I didn't want to see her."

Rila grinned. "Indeed. Then…what shall I do?"

"What do you mean?"

"Well…it's…," Rila mumbled. For once, she wasn't speaking her mind.

I was also at a loss for words.

"You fool!" Roje tried to head-butt me, but I smacked her away with a hand.

"Don't delude yourself into thinking you can hurt me. Now, what's suddenly gotten into you?"

"Lord Rileyla means to say that she wants to go with you!"

When I looked at her, Rila turned her face away.

"Roje Sandsong, she hasn't said anything like that," I stated.

"That's why you're a fool! An oaf!"

"R-Roje, it's fine. You will make me embarrassed if you declare it so openly…"

"See! You've made Lord Rileyla uncomfortable!"

The elf tried to strike my head several times with the ladle, but I blocked it with my hand.

"Don't shout. *You're* the reason she's embarrassed," I countered.

"She just wants to hear you say, 'Come with me'!"

Another ladle strike came flying in, so I stole Roje's weapon and gave her a whack on the head.

"Ouch!"

"...Is that true, Rila?" I questioned.

Her voice a whisper, she replied, "I am also curious to know how Maylee has fared. Though it was only for a short time, we did live together."

"In that case, you can come with me."

"Hey, human, I've told you multiple times now that is not what she meant! Lord Rileyla means to say—"

Quivering, Roje left the room, then immediately returned and thrust a book at me.

"Lord Rileyla read this romance novel, and it resonated with her! There's a scene similar to this, and she wanted the same experience, then today that was exactly what—"

Come to think of it, Rila *had* obtained something from Milia in secret. Evidently, this was the mysterious object.

Rila's face turned scarlet, and she yelled, "Stoooop it! That's enough! Leave! How dare you tell him!"

"Hmph. It seems she has grown weary of you, human."

"I think she means you," I corrected.

"What?"

"Get out!"

"Lord Rileyla, why are you forcing me to leave? I explained

Chapter 2

everything to this human since you are so modest! What have I done to deserve punishment?!"

"Just go!!"

Roje looked like an abandoned dog as Rila shoved her out the door. With that done, Rila cleared her throat and took a seat.

"So will you come with me?" I asked.

Was *that* all she'd wanted?

"Mm. I see. Then I shall accompany you…" Rila nodded, her face flushing again just slightly.

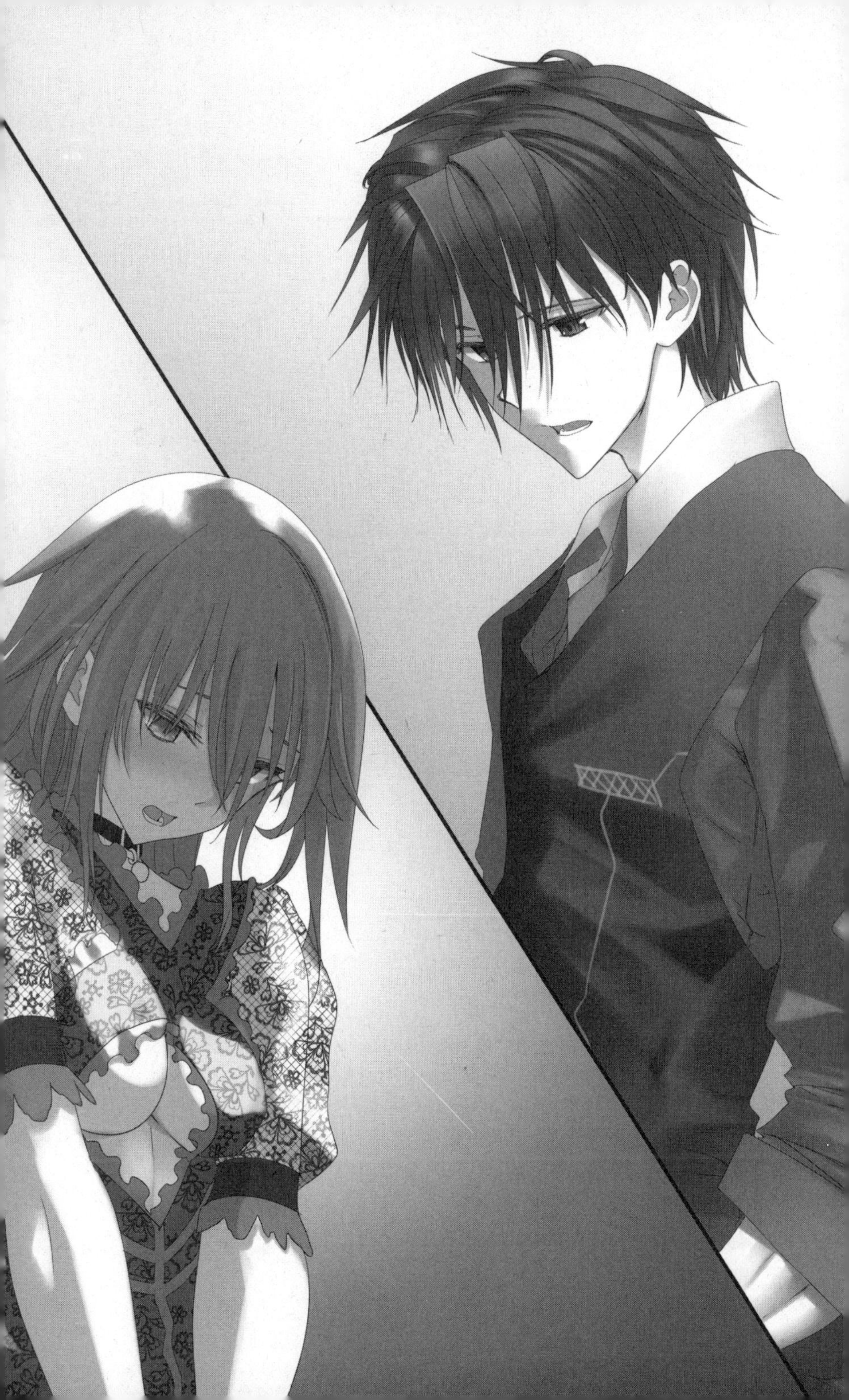

3
To the Duchy of Bardenhawk, Part I

The clatter of a carriage prompted the guild workers to pause their efforts. Few came to the office that way. It had to be someone from the capital.

"Fine work today, everyone," I heard someone say. I glanced over to find the guild master, Tallow, making his way in and walking toward me. I more or less understood what he had come for. He wanted to discuss sending guild employees out to Bardenhawk, just as King Randolph had told me.

Since some workers recognized Tallow and others didn't, half of them were frozen with surprise, and the others were looking on in curiosity.

"Stop right there, mister. What are you doing? Why did you barge in like that? Brawny, aren'tcha? Are you hoping to be an adventurer?" Maurey wasted no time questioning Tallow. Since the guild master had worked his way up from being an adventurer, Maurey wasn't too off the mark.

I was curious to see how this would play out.

"What? I don't think he is."

"Yeah, I'm pretty sure that's…"

My colleagues were whispering among themselves.

"And you can't just go around saying 'fine work today' like you're their senior manager. Hasn't anyone taught you proper work etiquette?"

"Ha-ha-ha. Well, I suppose you're right."

Maurey snorted. "Hmph. So long as you get the idea. Oh, you silly adventurer applicants. Sheesh."

"He's putting up with Maurey's condescending attitude?!"

"Th-this is a disaster! Someone, anyone, hurry and call the branch manager."

"Branch Managerrrrrr!"

As a stir ran through the office, Milia called in an airy voice, "Oh, so we have an aspiring adventurer? Please make your way to the reception—"

Clearly, she didn't recognize Tallow, either.

She turned to me.

"Mr. Roland, we have a potential adventurer. Could you help him at the front desk?"

It seemed that Tallow had no intention of correcting them. "If you could please," he said while nodding to me.

"…Please don't toy with the employees, you fool."

"Ha-ha-ha-ha."

"Do you know him, Mr. Roland? What a relief," Milia said as she grinned at Tallow. Maurey looked peeved.

"He's one of Roland's buds? Sheesh. You're not doing this right. Can't even mind his manners. Teaching adventurers is supposed to

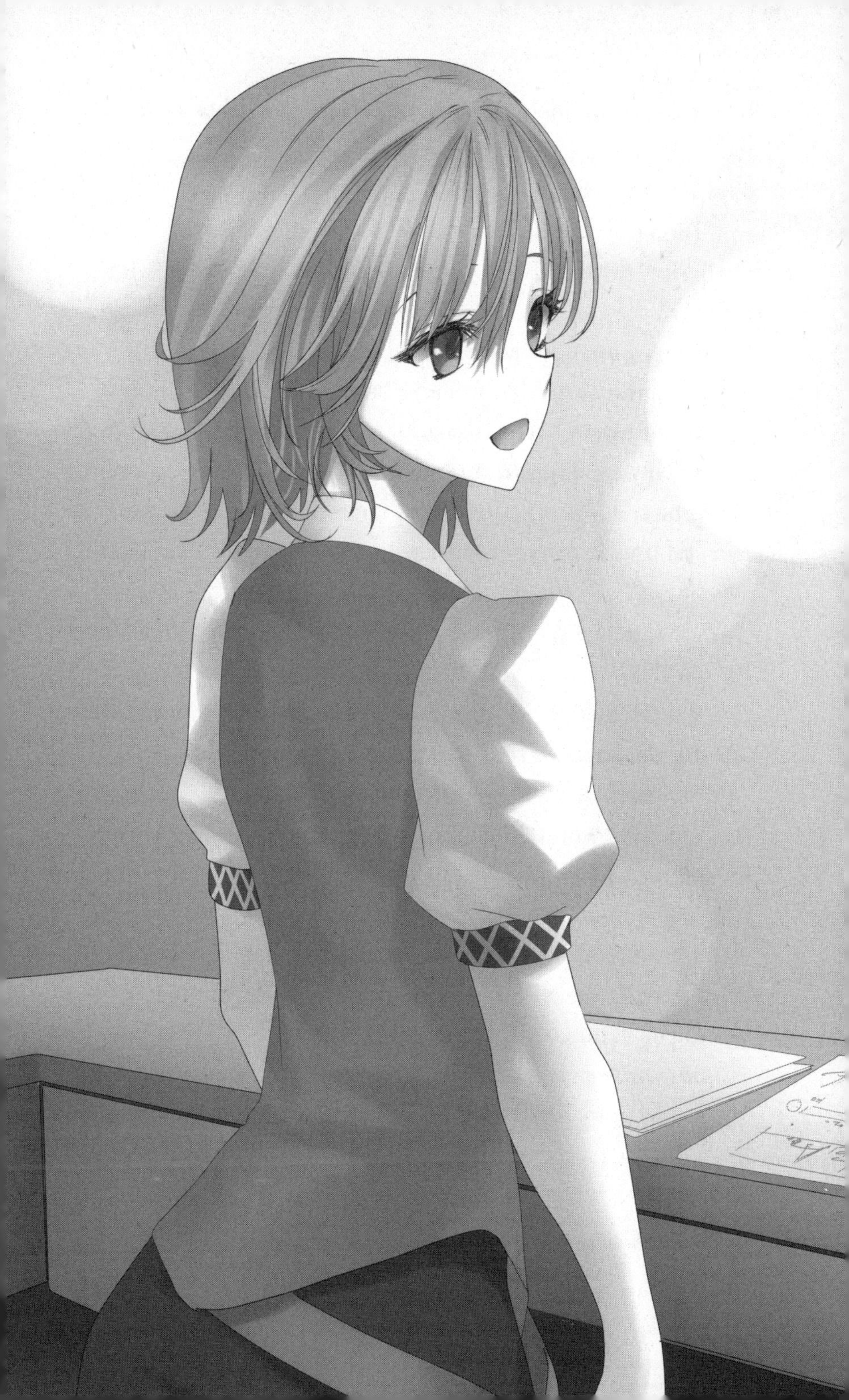

be part of your job as a staffer, y'know. You gotta revise your methods."

"Yes, understood," I replied.

"Ha-ha-ha. Roland, *the* Roland is...being *scolded!*"

"Tsk. This is only happening because you're toying with the workers."

"Come now, don't glare at me like that."

Iris quickly came out from the back room.

"Guild Master! Wh-what brings you here today? Oh, and I'm so sorry my employees didn't recognize you!"

Milia and Maurey both looked up from their seats in astonishment at the brawny man they had mistaken for an aspiring adventurer.

"Now, now, I don't mind. I have something quick to talk with Roland about."

"Branch Manager, a little incident like that isn't enough to agitate the guild master, so there's no need to worry," I assured her.

"R-really?" Iris still seemed dubious.

"I'm *soooo* sorry!" Maurey slipped out of his chair and prostrated himself on the ground.

"Uh, um. I'm also sorry..." Milia stood and bobbed her head.

"I can see that you're dedicated to your job. So keep up the good work." Tallow was mainly addressing Milia, but Maurey was looking up at him with glittering eyes.

He looks the same as the idiotic elf when Rila praises her.

"Come with me." I stood up from my seat and led the guild master to the reception room.

"I really can't approve of your rude reception, Argan."

"A proper guest wouldn't toy with the staff. Branch Manager, would you join us?"

"Huh? Me? Sure." Iris's eyes went wide, but she came with us nonetheless.

Tallow plunked himself down heavily on the sofa and sunk in. "Now, where shall we start?" he said.

"How about Bardenhawk's guild? I already heard about it from King Randolf."

Iris seemed puzzled as she looked at Tallow and me in turn.

"Ah yes, right. I have corresponded with Queen Leyte a number of times. In the future, she would like to do away with the borders between Felind and Bardenhawk, at least as far as the adventurers are concerned. That way, they'd be able to take quests from us and vice versa. Before anything else, though, we'd have to establish the guild in their country, and—" He explained the situation to Iris, who looked to have some difficulty following along.

"...And you want the personnel sent there...to be chosen by Roland?"

"To make things easier, we will consider this a quest from the Duchy of Bardenhawk, and we'll count it as a broadscale one, too. King Randolf himself requested it and put Roland in charge."

"So you're treating this as a quest where they've asked us to establish a guild system," I remarked. "I see. So you're leaving the hard part to me, then."

"Ha-ha-ha-ha. There's no need to put it like that. Still, you're the only person who's up to it. Especially with your 'Roland gang.'"

Chapter 3

"My what?"

What did he mean by that?

"You didn't know? I think that's what they call the adventurers you've treated well during quest arrangements and the ones you've passed in the tests," Iris explained matter-of-factly.

"Yes. That's right."

Even Iris knew about this?

"...What kind of sorry excuse for a name is that?" I was starting to get a headache. The Roland gang...? Was that supposed to be? A kind of construction crew?

"From what I've heard, they're well trained and willing to gather wherever you tell them to..."

"That's about the gist of it."

Apparently, this little band was centered around the adventurers I regularly helped.

After the three of us reviewed the general plans, Milia brought in some tea and gracefully bowed before leaving.

Tallow rubbed his chin. "So her name is Milia... She's rather cute. Seems the naive sort."

"I know you've had a penchant for her type since the old days," I said.

"Y-you don't mean to say you and Milia have already—" Tallow began, but I cut him off.

"Please don't get into vulgarities."

Iris laughed.

Hesitantly, Tallow asked, "Iris...is Roland just as popular here?"

"Yes."

"Hah. I see. Of course he would be. It's been that way for you since the war. They say all the gals in the mage unit were in love with you—every single one of them. The rumor went that you had a different woman visiting your camp every night. How many did you bed?"

There was a resounding thump as I kicked Tallow in the shin.

"Ouch!"

"You fool. We're with the branch manager, a woman. There's a time and a place."

"So how many? Maybe a dozen?"

"About half of the unit."

"What?! But they didn't even give me the time of day!"

"It's because you're loud, tactless, and unhygienic."

Women who could use magic came from nobility, for the most part. Being a mage was a status symbol in its own way. Many aristocrats would dedicate themselves to studying spells from their youth. A lot of the women in the war had been those low in the line of succession for family inheritances. I heard after the fact that most of them had married decorated knights, mages, and accomplished military officers.

"Oh, before I forget, here's your Plant Master license."

Tallow produced a badge from his pocket and set it on the desk as though it were an afterthought.

"You brought it just as I was beginning to forget about it," I replied.

"Few are able to earn one, so they take time to make," Tallow explained. "I'll leave you to pick the people for the broadscale quest. I believe Queen Leyte and Her Highness will likely assist you directly once you arrive."

Her Highness? Oh, he must mean Maylee.

I pinned on my Plant Master badge, and Tallow shooed Iris from the room so we could speak privately. He'd discussed crude things in front of her, so what could he possibly wish to talk about alone?

Tallow was silent for a while. Perhaps he was checking for people listening outside.

After Iris's footsteps faded, we started to hear the din of the office out front.

"Roland...," Tallow said in a hushed tone as he leaned forward across the table. I did the same and brought my ear close to him. "I have visited Bardenhawk many a time, and on one trip...I saw her..."

Out of all things he could have said, I wasn't expecting that.

I stared Tallow in the face, but it seemed he wasn't joking.

"You must be mistaken. You wouldn't be able to tell."

"That's what I figured, too, but... She frightens me, but to you, she's like a parent, right?"

"We can't be certain she's still there."

"I know."

"Why are you bringing this up now?"

"Bardenhawk is still in turmoil. They claim that they want to create a parliament, which means that normal citizens may soon carry power that was once exclusive to kings and queens. There's no shortage of people trying to use this mess to get up to no good in the shadows."

I recalled the contents of the letter I had found in the house in the mountains.

"This broadscale quest I'm taking *is* actually to set up a guild and manage it, right?" I questioned.

"If it was a case of mistaken identity on my part, then yes. By the way, I'm not sure when it was established, but word has it that Bardenhawk has a secret guild."

"Rumors such as those don't bode well."

"They're doing the exact opposite of our Adventurers Guild. They steal, kidnap, poach, smuggle contraband, and…assassinate."

"…And that's why you suspect it may truly be her?"

"Yes. I wouldn't tell you about this if I'd only caught a glimpse of her. I hope that none of this is related…"

"If there's one thing about you that I find admirable, it's that your intuition exceeds reason," I said.

"That's why I wanted *you* on this broadscale quest…"

"Fighting fire with fire. I see…"

Tallow's uneasiness was warranted, considering the situation.

He stood silently, patted me on the shoulder, and left the room.

"Hey, Neal, come over here for a moment."

I called over Neal, who had come by while I was working, and had him sit across from me.

"B-boss…wh-what is it? You seem different from usual…"

The moment I caught sight of the man, I'd accidentally let Roland the assassin show through. I hastily returned to being the guild worker, Mr. Argan.

I was impressed by Roger, who had come in with Neal. As soon as he'd realized there was something different about me, he'd quietly hidden away.

"Mr. Neal, do you know about the 'Roland gang'?" I inquired.

"Huh? Well, I don't just know about it…heh-heh-heh."

"What's that supposed to me?"

"I'm the one who set it up, boss!"

"*Tsk…*"

"Did you just cluck your tongue at me?!"

After a sigh, I told him I was heading to Bardenhawk for a broadscale quest.

"What?! Then, boss…does that mean you won't be at the Lahti branch for a while?"

"That's right. I think I'll be out for roughly three months. Now, about that primary matter. There aren't many adventurers over in Bardenhawk. Even if we have quests, we won't be able to establish a guild unless we have people to do them."

"I suppose so."

"If you were to call together this embarrassingly named Roland gang, how many people do you suppose would gather? I'd like them to come with me to tackle quests in Bardenhawk, if possible."

"Oh, are you asking me…for a favor, boss?!"

Roger, who'd been listening, quickly butted in, "Leave it to me, boss! I can gather thirty…no, fifty people for you!"

"Hey, the boss was asking *me* to help him!"

"Then I'm counting on you. Please ask anyone willing to help to head over to Bardenhawk's capital, Izaria. We're planning on creating the first guild in the duchy there."

Since Leyte would be helping us, that likely wouldn't cause any friction.

"It used to be occupied by the demon lord's army. There's less public order compared to here, so make sure to be vigilant. I think the quests will have lower payouts, as well…"

Since it was a broadscale quest, the adventurers would ultimately receive a reward, but I couldn't tell them the exact amount yet, so I didn't mention it.

"That's fine, boss. Our group was founded out of our devotion and loyalty to you!" Neal said.

I didn't put much faith in words like *devotion* or *loyalty*, but my observations of Roje did suggest those concepts were real.

"I'm going to gather way more people than you, Roger!"

"Neal, looks like it's finally my time to shine."

"Are there really that many people in the group?" I asked.

I didn't feel like I'd actually passed that many adventurers on tests or arranged that many quests.

"You probably just don't remember them all, but there are plenty. Lots of folks feel indebted to you."

"We'll get you adventurers totaling in the triple digits!"

Neal and Roger were both incredibly excited. Once they left, I began selecting staff.

I needed us to be able to do our usual work in Bardenhawk… Iris had told everyone about the broadscale quest and the gist of what it entailed during our morning meeting. Maybe that was why I felt like there were so many eyes on me.

"Mr. Roland, I'll have you know that I've been here longer than you. I have quite a bit of experience, too." Milia appealed to me

Chapter 3   79

directly. Additionally, I felt a sort of unspoken pressure coming from all of the female staffers.

"A business trip that lasts months!"

"And we get to work together to overcome difficulties!"

"And after sharing in all the ups and downs, the two of us might fall in love…"

"It's the perfect path towards workplace romance!"

The stares were intense.

I realized I'd sensed similar gazes on me before—the eyes of carnivores.

"How is it going?" called Iris. "I'm sure you're having trouble choosing people."

"Yes. But I've filled around seventy percent of the positions already. Fortunately, there are some adventurers willing to help, too."

"Are there? I'm glad to hear that."

If I was going, Dey would certainly follow.

She was versatile and had keen battle prowess. Among all the adventurers I knew, she was likely the one I could count on the most.

Guess it's time to ask her formally…

"Branch Manager," I said.

"Hmm? What is it? Oh, I can recommend some employees I think would be good fits."

"Branch Manager, would you please come with me?"

After a moment, Iris's face turned red.

"M-me?!"

"Yes. Tallow...I mean, the guild master, has already given his permission."

"...Um, uh...I-I...I suppose that'd b-be okay..." She was fidgeting tremendously, but still agreed.

"Thank you. I haven't been in an administrative position before, so I think it would be right to bring someone with experience."

"Y-you invited me because I'm the branch manager? I see...yes, of course...of course you would."

Iris narrowed her eyes, looking pained. Meanwhile, the other female staff members were growing restless.

"Miss Milia, would you come as well?" I inquired.

"Absolutelyyyy!"

She was very enthusiastic, which worked great for me.

"In which case... I guess your only remaining choice is to bring me, right? Since you haven't got any other options," Maurey remarked.

He seemed to have been waiting for me to ask him along, but I'd already requested two different male employees who I knew much better, and they both gave their okays. My final picks were a pair from the capital's western branch.

Including Milia and me, there were six normal guild workers. That would probably be sufficient. If there was anything extra, I was confident that Iris could help out.

"But Mr. Roland, isn't Bardenhawk still dangerous?" Milia questioned.

Iris beat me to the punch, answering, "The capital has improved significantly. You shouldn't be in any more danger while working there than you would be here. Most importantly, because you work with Roland, you'll be able to live in the castle during the trip."

All of the staff and adventurers who were listening let out an "*Ohhhhhh.*"

"...So does that mean Mr. Argan has a connection to the royalty there?"

"Probably?"

"He's in good with the King of Felind, too."

"Maybe someday he'll join a royal family..."

"He genuinely might..."

Milia's eyes were glittering. "A castle! Maybe we'll see the moments leading up to a prince and princess falling in love?!"

I shook my head. "That sort of scenario only exists in your imagination, so you're better off just forgetting about it."

Iris and Shane, the interim branch manager, were talking things over and making decisions.

"Seriously? Like, seriously. Am I on the stairway to a promotion? I might get one! That must be why I didn't get asked to come along. I see. That's what's happening." Maurey was mumbling loudly to himself about things that would never come to pass.

I hadn't objected to the candidate Iris had selected for interim branch manager. I'd wanted to bring Shane, who'd taken me drinking with him in the past, but everyone else would feel better having him around. He was a senior staff member and had dependable skills.

"I'm entrusting things to you, Shane, while I'm out."

"All right. You got it."

Maurey, who had been quivering, finally broke down into tears. "Whyyy?! Why didn't you pick me?!"

Everyone looked at him with contempt. They all let out a sigh, too.

"And you didn't even take me with you to Bardenhawk!"

Iris pressed her temple to hold a headache at bay.

I wanted to tell him we didn't select him because he acted like this.

Maurey wasn't the type we could invite to someone's castle without keeping a constant eye on him. We weren't going to leave the guild in his hands while we were out, either.

"Mr. Maurey, we can't bring you along because you're too exceptional."

"Hunh?! What?! You can't?!"

"The branch manager, Miss Milia, two others, and I are going to be out for a while, so there won't be enough people working… We need great guild employees to stay here and hold down the fort," I said.

"I-I see, so that's what happened! I get it now!" he replied, excited.

"We're counting on you to keep an eye on things while we're away, Mr. Maurey."

"Of course!"

He was a tiresome man, but once you knew how to manipulate him, it was easy.

"Hmm? W-wait a sec. Then shouldn't I be the interim branch

manager?! Shane and I started working at around the same time...! Actually, I think I'm a little better than he is!"

The looks from all around the room told him that wasn't remotely true. The only thing Maurey had to be proud about was his score in the Plant Master qualification test, although I'd beaten both his time and his grade.

"What we need from a manager and a staffer is different," I told him. "You're our star player, Mr. Maurey."

"Now that's a difficult order to follow...but I guess that means I'm the right man for the job!"

Maurey was a fool. The slightest bit of praise was enough to convince him.

He was a chump.

With that, the personnel selection for the broadscale quest was complete. We decided on the time we'd leave, and I told everyone where we were headed.

◆

Using the Gate I'd set up the night before, I headed to the Duchy of Bardenhawk with everyone.

It was a small country on the coast south of Felind.

It had a warm climate and was famous for its marine products and fruit. We had rushed to the outskirts of Izaria, the capital. They were still repairing the castle walls that had likely burned down during the nation's collapse. There were many scorched sections visible here and there.

If we continued south, we would hit the former country of Yorvensen…a region that the demon lord's army had taken as a foothold for invading human territory. I'd heard that since the demon lord's army left, it was no longer acknowledged as a country.

"I see. So you've been making round trips whenever you wanted between the capital and your home using this magic."

"That's exactly right," I replied.

Rila, Roje, and Dey would be following us later using Roje's Gate magic. The adventurers Neal and Roger were gathering would likely assemble in the coming days.

I had told everyone that Maylee was Bardenhawk's princess.

"Wooow! So Maylee lives here in the capital, then…" Milia, who was carrying a giant pack, had a twinkle in her eyes.

The male staff members were looking all over the place. The sudden jump likely didn't feel real to them.

"I wonder if things will be all right while I'm away from the Lahti branch," Iris wondered.

"I'm sure it'll be okay," I told her.

If the Roland gang, or whatever they called themselves, were making their way here, our office would see fewer adventurers for a while.

"Th-this is my first time living in another country… I wonder if things will be okay."

"S-same for me…"

"And me…"

"Me too…"

Chapter 3 85

Apparently, none of my coworkers had previously spent time outside their homeland.

"Bardenhawk's customs are no different from our own. Many of Felind's construction guild members are working here, so you can spend rins just fine. You shouldn't run into much trouble at all."

The only differences were the warmer climate and the proximity to the sea.

We were stopped at the castle gate and had to explain our situation to the guards.

"...I didn't hear anything about this," one said to us.

"We're here on orders from Queen Leyte and King Felind," I stated.

The two guards exchanged looks and shook their heads.

"You seem even more suspicious now that you've named the queen. And what even is an Adventurers Guild?"

"We're not suspicious at all…" I had to wonder why no one had informed them of the situation. "Please call your superiors. Nothing will come out of this."

"Why would we waste time doing that?" one guard snapped.

"If you keep pushing this, mister, we won't be able to keep quiet about what you're doing," one guard said sharply, then they both glowered as though to intimidate us.

I wish we'd had a contract or the like, but Tallow hadn't mentioned anything of the sort, which led me to think they'd let us right in.

My conversation with the guards had reached a standstill. That was when an unexpected commotion began within the castle gates. The guards' door next to the main gate was flung open.

"Oh, you're here! Rolaaaand!"

Maylee, dressed appropriately for a princess, was hurrying over to me at the quickest pace she could manage.

The two guards turned when they heard her voice.

""Y-Your Highness?!""

Flustered, they knelt swiftly.

Maylee charged into me and gave me a hug.

"Roland, welcome."

"Thanks. We just arrived."

I hugged her back as she clung to my hips.

"Why haven't you come in yet?" she asked.

"It seems there was a little mistake."

Maylee tilted her head to the side quizzically.

"Mr. Roland, I am glad to see you've made it all this way after your journey."

Leyte emerged from the same door Maylee had.

""Your Majesty, too?!""

The two surprised guards began whispering to each other.

"Wh-who is this guy...?"

"Don't ask me..."

"H-Her Majesty came all the way here to greet him personally..."

"What's going to happen now?"

Iris, Milia, and the other staffers were all on one knee and bowing their heads.

"It's been a long time, Lady Leyte. We just arrived," I greeted.

Chapter 3   87

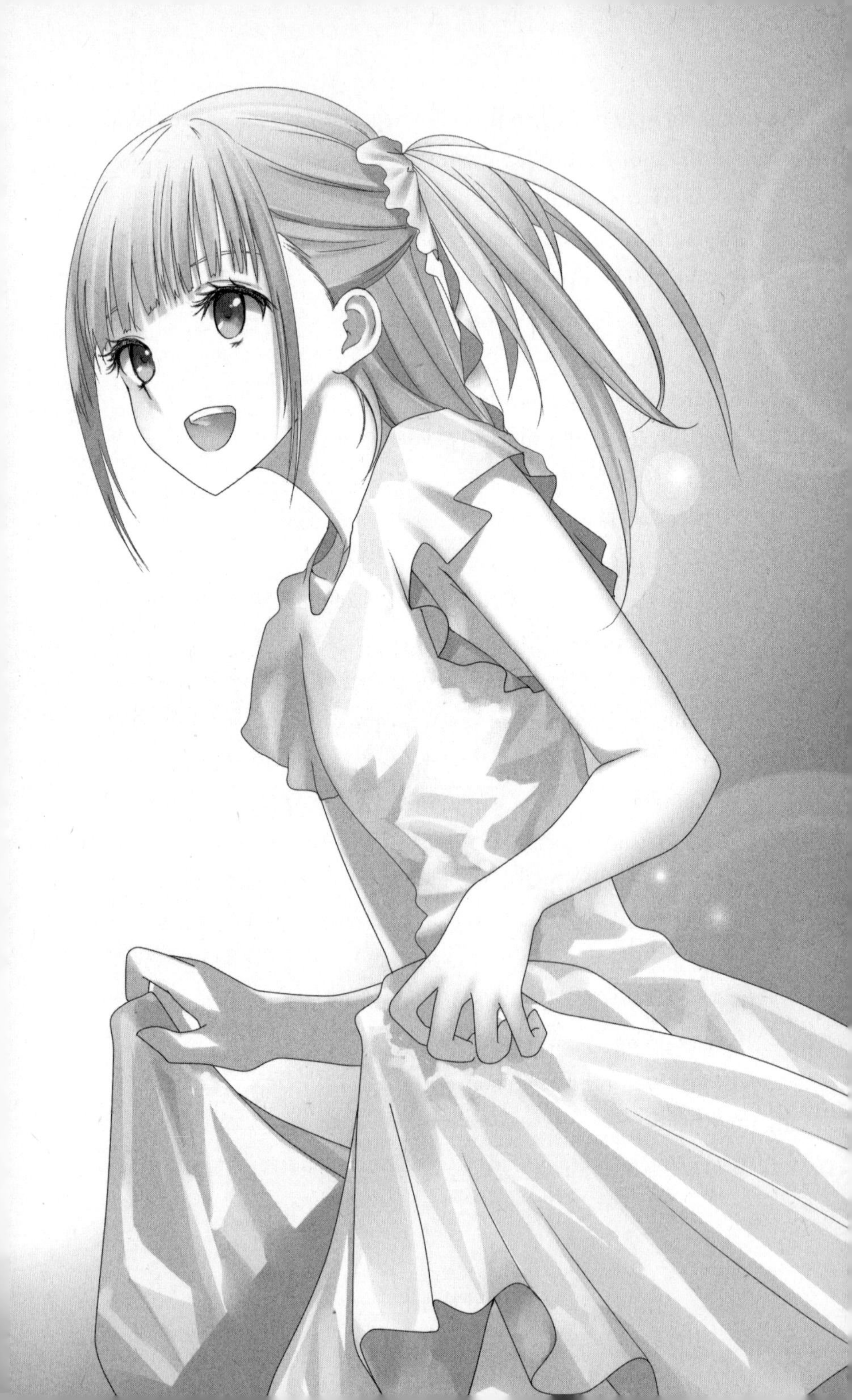

"Is that right?"

Maylee gave my neck a squeeze and wouldn't let go. "I'll show you around the castle!" she exclaimed. "Then we'll eat together and play in my room!"

"You've grown into a fine princess, Maylee," I praised.

"Hee-hee. Here, look." She produced a knife in a case from behind her back.

"That's the one I bought for you from the adventurer exam..."

"Uh-huh. I've kept it with me ever since."

"There are some who would be frightened if they saw a princess carrying around something like that."

"It's fine."

Leyte laughed as she watched our exchange. "Alias, Mr. Roland came here for work. Take care not to bother him."

"Ugh." Maylee looked dissatisfied as she groaned.

"Mr. Roland, did you encounter any inconveniences during your trip?" Leyte inquired.

The two guards trembled and immediately stepped back.

"I wouldn't go so far as to call it an inconvenience, but...I do feel as though some information was lost in transit."

"As I was waiting, I realized the gates hadn't opened. I was certain I'd told them to expect you, though." Leyte's words prompted the guards to begin sweating.

"Ma...maybe it was that...?" one suggested.

"That what? Oh—you mean *that*?!" responded the other.

"I-I heard that visitors were coming from Felind...but I'd assumed they would be royalty..."

Chapter 3 89

Leyte let out a long sigh. "These are our guests," she said. "I expressly invited them here. Did you intend to send them away?"

""S-sorry!"" exclaimed the two guards.

"You're saying it to the wrong person," Leyte chided.

""We're so sorry.""

The two men prostrated themselves before me.

"I must also apologize," Leyte added.

"No, you and the guards have no need to go that far. It was only a misunderstanding. I'm sure they would've let us in before long."

Leyte gave me a questioning look. "Do you really think so?"

I nodded.

The two guards looked ready to bawl at any moment.

I silently gestured to them with my head, which prompted them to bow in gratitude.

"…Mr. Roland is so cool."

"He really is."

Milia and Iris were having their own little conversation behind me.

"Izaria is modest compared to Felind's capital, Finlan, but thanks to you, we have been able to rebuild. I welcome all of you from the Adventurers Guild. Please come in."

Leyte motioned with her hands, prompting the gate to slowly open.

There was a banquet and a party to celebrate our arrival.

We were being treated as state guests, which made the whole affair a bit stuffy, but not to the point of inconvenience.

Following the festivities, we devoted several days to inspecting the area where the new guild headquarters would be established. We then met with the junior- and mid-level government officials.

The biggest issue was that they didn't seem to understand what quests or adventurers were.

"Ugh! Roland isn't playing with me at all!" Maylee, who had come by my room with her lady-in-waiting, pouted.

I had mostly left the princess to her own devices. Honestly, I really didn't have any time to spend with her.

Rila and the others had also arrived, but they weren't staying in the castle because they weren't guild employees. Instead, they had found lodgings at a nearby inn.

Since the demon lord's army had once occupied this nation, we had decided it would be better for Rila not to be in her demon form. At present, she was a black cat.

"You have a day off today, right?"

"Yes. Want to tag along with me, Maylee? I'm going to look around the town with Rila."

"...Isn't that a, um...one of those things? A date?"

"I think it's slightly different from a date. Also, Rila wants to see you."

"But then Rila will be in the way. Hmph." Maylee pouted and turned away.

"She won't."

"Fine..."

It seemed Maylee had become precocious since I'd seen her last. I told her lady-in-waiting I was taking the princess out, and we did not need a guard. Iris and Milia were apparently having a look around the town, so I expected to spot them somewhere.

"I'll show you around, okay?" Maylee said to me.

"How dependable you are," I replied. "Have you been continuing your training?"

"Yup! I'm really fast at the Back Slash now."

I let go of her hand and moved some distance away.

I motioned for Maylee to come closer, and after she understood my intentions, she readied her knife.

Thud, thud, thud, thud. She quickly ran at me. She *had* grown swifter.

"Back Sla—"

I turned toward Maylee, who had made her way behind me, and grabbed her by the face.

"Shhaaah?!"

"Your footsteps are too loud," I told her. "You still have a long way to go. Trying to take someone by surprise from behind is meaningless if they can detect you."

"Waaaaah! You're stupid, Roland!" Maylee slapped my arm and stomped away down the hall.

"You really are still a child."

I shrugged and followed after the grumpy princess.

"Ah-ha-ha-ha. Why, Maylee hasn't changed in the slightest."

Once we met Rila outside the castle and I told her what had happened, she began to laugh. Maylee didn't seem amused, though.

"I'd definitely be able to do it to you, Rila," she said.

"Oh? You would do well not to underestimate me. You may attack anytime you wish."

We were drinking juice at an empty eatery. The liquid was red, so I'd initially thought it would be tomato, but the flavor suggested it was some variety of strong-tasting orange.

"I can handle you with just the Slash I came up with, Rila."

"Hmm? Is that some new technique?"

"That's right. I hit really fast from the front."

I cocked an eyebrow. "Maylee, isn't that the same as a normal strike?"

"That doesn't matter!"

Maylee swung her legs wildly as she sipped the red orange juice through a straw.

"How are Roje and Dey doing?" I asked.

Rila replied in a whisper, "The demon lord's army once occupied this land. It seems they are checking for 'forgotten' things for the time being."

"I see. I'm sure they'll have better luck here than in Felind. Especially regarding lost monsters."

Rila quietly nodded several times. If we were to gather quests from around the area, many of them would surely involve vanquishing creatures of the former demon lord's army. As the three of us sat and drank, I discussed work a bit.

"Our goal is to be here for three months, but there'll undoubtedly be some trips back and forth. Honestly, our target time might be too short."

"You're only here for three months, Roland…?" Maylee asked.

Chapter 3

"It may be a little longer than that."

"You should stay forever. You can be a big shot at the guild."

"That would cause a few problems," I replied. I stroked Maylee's hair with a faint smile.

The adult world was wearisome.

"It seems they're having difficulty understanding what quests and adventurers are. I myself had not grasped it initially, either," Rila commented.

When I thought about it, we had begun this undertaking thinking such concepts were obvious, but to the uninitiated, it all sounded like esoteric jargon.

During an earlier meeting, the junior officials had seemed slightly concerned.

"So...I understand that adventurers go on quests, but...why would they help with the civilians' problems around town? Shouldn't they be out doing other things?" one of them had said.

Iris and the other staffer had given explanations and broken down the concepts, but the majority of people from Bardenhawk we met with had difficulty accepting it all.

It would take a bit more time for the new ideas to permeate the country.

Maylee finished her juice and stood up.

I tried to pay.

"That will be three thousand rins."

"Quite a hefty price," I said.

The bearded man who owned the place looked apologetic as he scratched his cheek.

"I'm sorry, sir. I almost want to say that I can't accept payment from the princess."

"Normally, wouldn't one of these be about five hundred rins?" Maylee pointed out, which made the man look dispirited, and he lowered his head.

"You're right. However, the blood oranges we need have increased in price... It seems that there have been more monster attacks on the road to the capital, and because of all the protection fees and whatnot, costs have increased..."

This was it. I immediately put on my guild worker face and assumed a formal air.

"Would you like to consult with me about that issue you are having?"

"Huh? Can I?"

"Yes. Princess Alias will deal with your problem."

Rila and Maylee seemed to have also caught on.

"I-I'll do it! I'll fix your issue!"

This would be her first quest, a makeup for the one she hadn't been able to do that day.

If there was a person in need, a guild worker, and an adventurer, that meant a quest.

"Oh, well, I couldn't ask the princess to do something like that..."

"We will go with her, so please don't worry," I responded.

"Hmmm," the man muttered pensively. Eventually, he accepted my proposal.

"Well then, let's hear more about the problem."

We returned to our seats after having just left them and got the details from the man.

"You said the blood oranges that you use for juice have increased in price because monsters prowl the roads?" I questioned.

"Yes. That fruit's the only thing we order from afar, but other shops have it much worse."

It seemed this was a typical slaying quest.

"If we're able to solve your problem, would you allow us to supply a consultation box and some paper for writing troubles down on?"

"I wouldn't mind that… Just who are you, lad?"

"I'm a guild worker. It's my job to act as a mediator for people who need their problems solved by others."

"Ah yes, I recall something about other countries offering services like that."

The traveling merchant who sold the oranges came by the capital periodically, but they'd just visited a few days ago, so it would be a while before they came back.

Normally, we would conduct an inspection of the place to find out what kinds of monsters there were and what the situation was like so we could set up an appropriate rank and reward. I would be tagging along for the quest this time, though, so there was no need.

There wouldn't be any issues, regardless of the area's state or what creatures there were.

We examined a map charting the route the merchant used. It seemed they stopped in multiple settlements, and they were frequently attacked between the last town and the capital.

"If they are targeting the food, the monster may be intelligent," Rila whispered.

"Maylee, this will be your first battle. You're not scared, are you?"

Maylee let out a snort. "I'm not scared! I'll go *zwoosh, swoosh, swoosh* with my Back Slash! And beat them!"

That was the spirit.

It seemed Maylee was something of a darling among the people who lived in the city.

Once we left, the man watched us go with evident worry.

"Princess, please do be careful."

"I will. Thank you, mister."

Maylee gave him an enthusiastic wave and followed after Rila and me in high spirits.

4
To the Duchy of Bardenhawk, Part II

After setting out from the capital, we followed a long road.

"If they do that, then I'll use this!"

Swoosh.

"And…if they do this, I'll do this!"

Swoosh.

Maylee was absorbed in whatever she was doing.

"Have you fought since leaving us?" Rila inquired.

"No. I've been with my mother the whole time, and all we do is look around the town together."

"So I supposed that makes this your first battle."

Rila was looking at Maylee as though the girl was a baby chick.

"What about you, Roland? What was your first battle like?" asked Maylee.

"Hmm. Yes, I would like to know as well," Rila said.

"It wasn't interesting at all," I said. That did little to deter them, however, so I recounted the story.

"Everything went as planned, and there weren't any unexpected events. I came into contact with the target and killed them within twenty seconds. I used one of the four methods of retreat I had prepared to get away... That's it."

Rila and Maylee seemed utterly unimpressed and let down.

"'Twas uninteresting."

"Boooring!"

"I told you, didn't I?"

At some point during our chat, we came across a mark in the path.

"Do you think a big ant could have left this behind?" Rila suggested.

"...I think it's likely," I replied.

"What's that?" Maylee tilted her head, confused, so I explained it to her.

"It's a type of insect monster. They make nests underground and can grow as large as a medium-sized dog," I explained.

Rila added, "The queen sits in the nest, and the servant big ants bring her food."

"There's a queen?"

"That's right," I answered. "...If they made a nest nearby, it's likely they'll attack."

Found it. It was a short distance ahead. The big ants were gathered around the corpses of three monsters.

"There they are, Maylee. Do you want to dispatch them?" I said.

"Ew... Th-they don't look like normal ants..."

To the young girl, the creatures must have seemed giant. There were undoubtedly many more big ants underground that surely would have made her cover her eyes if she saw them.

"R-Roland, can we really kill them…?"

"I can. But I'm a guild worker, and you're an adventurer with a provisional license. You've been judged to have more than enough mana and combat skills to handle this."

The big ants tore at the corpses with their jaws and used their sharp front legs to skewer the flesh.

They were slow to move. As long as Maylee kept an eye on their jaws and sicklelike feet, she would be able to defeat them without issue.

Unlike archery or spells, assassination techniques required getting in close to a target. Maylee's only weapons were her knife and herself. Drawing first blood wouldn't necessarily win this. She had to kill them with the initial blow. Doing that would test her grit and courage more than any training.

"These things have to be the ones attacking merchants as they pass by. Would you rather not do it? Adventurers I know very well will be here soon enough. You can leave it to them if you prefer," I remarked.

Maylee had to be around the same age as Lina, possibly even a year older. And while I'd trained her, she was still a princess. During training, she did okay, but a real battle could still be too much for her.

Or so I had thought, but Maylee's eyes still had determination in them.

"Maylee, take a close look. Soon, two of them will be moving away, leaving one on its own."

"O-okay…"

"Keep your cool. They're much weaker than you and me."

I could hear her swallow nervously. Rila was anxiously watching Maylee this whole time. I sensed Maylee was preparing herself for the fight. I'd considered coaching her through it, but it seemed that wouldn't be necessary.

Maylee ran directly at the big ant that was still occupied with the cadavers. Her Back Slash, which still had a long way to go as far as I was concerned, was more than enough of a threat to any monster. Maylee appeared well acquainted with the movements.

Hmm. Looks like this is settled, then.

"B-bash Lash!"

She'd flubbed the line.

The big ant suddenly turned around.

"*Kree?*"

Despite botching the attack name, Maylee's blade still pierced the big ant, carving through its head.

Zwoosh.

The weapon made a satisfying noise as she sliced through the monster.

"*Kree...kree...*"

The massive insect twitched several times, then stopped moving. Maylee's shoulders dropped in a release of tension as she turned to me.

"I killed it... Rolaaand! I killed it!"

Thud, thud, thud. Her footsteps were heavy as she ran over and latched on to me.

"That was a good cut," I told her.

"Wasn't it?" Maylee giggled as I petted her head and praised her.

I thought she would be wise to stop saying the name of her technique, though.

"Based on what I can see in the vicinity, there are around thirty more big ants nearby. I'm counting on you, Maylee."

"Huh?" The princess's face stiffened.

"Uh… Weren't there only two left?"

"Maylee. If you don't defeat the monsters attacking the traders, everyone will be in trouble," I reminded her.

"Uhh…"

Whether it was because they were hungry or not, I couldn't say, but the big ants started crawling out from a nest hole.

The big ants themselves were nothing to worry about, however.

"It looks like the queen will be making an appearance," Rila commented, as though spectating some distant event.

The gigantic queen emerged from underground, digging away the soil around her with her front legs.

"*Kreeee!*"

There we had it—the queen ant.

"Eep! Yikes! I-it's so biiig…," Maylee cried as she cowered in fear. This would be somewhat difficult for her. Since she was unused to seeing monsters, the queen must have seemed massive.

"Lord Rileylaaaa!" someone called.

I turned and saw Roje and Dey waving at us as they approached.

"You two came at just the right time," I said.

"Did something bad happen, Lord Rileyla?" Roje asked. Dey seemed curious as well.

Despite the queen ant before them, they calmly inquired about what was going on.

"Would you please help this girl, Maylee, defeat the big ants?" Rila requested.

"Is this *the* Maylee...?" Roje stared at the girl, who hid behind my back.

"Stop that, you perverted elf. Don't scare her."

"I'm not."

"Dey, would you mind lending a hand? It seems I can't trust Roje Sandsong to do it," I said.

Naturally, the elf was furious. "What did you just say?!"

"Hee-hee. Of course. What an adorable child. Why, I could eat her right up."

"There you have it, Maylee. These two women will assist you," I told her.

"O-okay... It's nice to meet you."

"And you," Dey replied.

"Fine, I'll do it. But only because Lord Rileyla told me to. This is a special favor to her."

Roje was just as troublesome as usual.

"Let's go beat up those ants, shall we?" Dey took Maylee's hand and started walking toward the enemy.

"Your palm is really cold, ma'am."

"Oh dear, is it? That's because I'm already dead, so I'm as cold as a banana in the middle of winter."

"???"

Maylee clearly didn't understand what Dey meant by that, saving us the trouble of a lengthy explanation.

Honestly, Dey didn't seem like a great influence as far as teaching Maylee was concerned. She was a walking corpse, after all.

"Hey, vampire! You took the kid without even consulting me! *I* was asked to help her!"

"Oh my. It looks like we have a very noisy elf on our hands." Dey fended off Roje's objection with a nonchalant remark.

The two made for an unexpectedly good comedic pair.

"So is the master going to simply watch as his favorite pupil does all the work?" Rila teased me with a laugh.

It annoyed me that she knew what I would be doing, but that was fine.

"Hee-hee! It's so fun to trample the weak!"

Dey was off waving her bloodsucking spear all about, slaying big ants.

"Hey, you'd better make sure to actually help the girl!" Roje scolded.

Next to them, Maylee had her knife at the ready and was attacking the insect monsters, defeating them one at a time.

She seemed to be doing just fine.

Meanwhile, the queen ant was making a terrible screeching noise while stabbing big ants and eating them.

"That hardly seems like a fitting end considering they were bringing her food all this time," I commented. Then I activated my skill, Unobtrusive.

In the blink of an eye, I was running up the queen ant's back.

I didn't have a weapon of any sort. Even if I plunged my arm straight into her body, she was too large for me to inflict much damage.

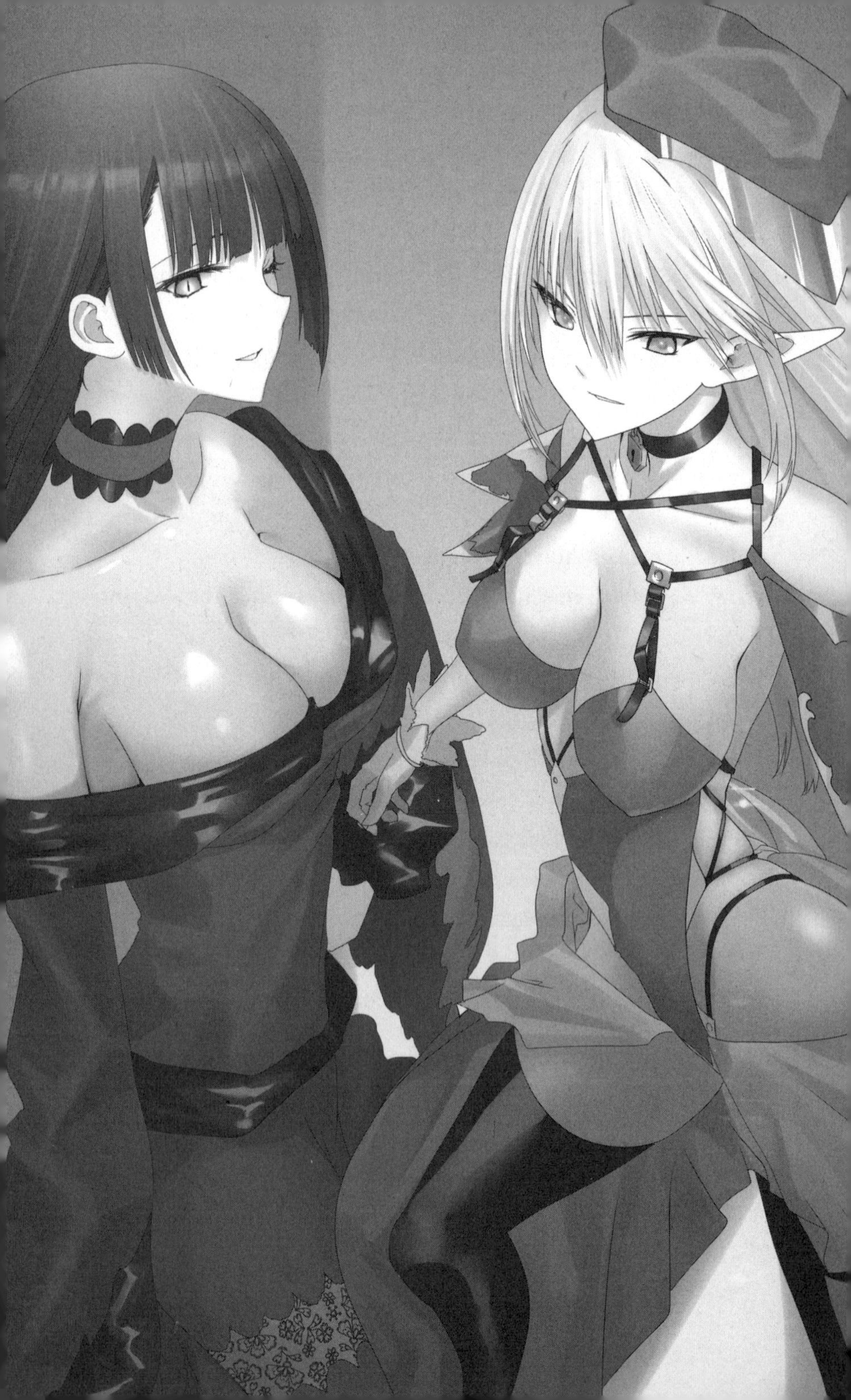

I delivered a karate chop to the neck.

A standard physical assault wouldn't be a fatal wound, of course. That was why I hit her as swiftly as I could and also imbued the wind my blows created with magic. I employed a smaller version of Magi Raegas, the technique that involved cloaking one's body in mana.

Shunk.

"*Kreeeeeeeeh?!*"

I gouged deep into the back of the queen ant's head. Now *that* was a mortal strike.

I'd thought it'd take at least two more hits, but the monster was unexpectedly soft. The queen went down, and I leaped off her.

Maylee, who had been engrossed in her own endeavors, let out a "*Wooow*" as she watched me with respect in her eyes.

"You got the big one, Roland!" she cheered.

"That you would, Master Roland. You were merciless and fantastic...," added Dey.

"Hey, you two! Don't stop! Guh, these blasted ants! Why are they only coming toward me—ahh?! I-it bit me in the behind!"

I felt bad for Roje, whose bottom was now half exposed, so I lent her a hand. That brought a swift end to the ant extermination.

After we finished, we returned to the capital and reported what had transpired to the man at the eatery.

"Wooow! You did that, Your Highness?"

"I did! I beat them!"

Chapter 4

The man's eyes went wide as Maylee stuck out her chest triumphantly.

"Maylee… Her Highness had special training, so she is adept at culling monsters," I added, since it was the truth.

With Bardenhawk's darling Maylee as our poster girl, these people would soon understand that adventurers could solve their problems.

"There is an old, three-story building in the central district. If you have any other troubles, please come visit the Adventurers Guild there."

"Whoa. Now that sounds convenient. Can get help with *any* sort of issue?"

"It depends on what you need, but there's no harm in asking. Consulting doesn't cost anything, but submitting a formal request requires a nominal fee."

"A fee, huh? Guess it's not a charity. So what's the bill this time, then…?"

"We were the ones to ask you about the trouble, so no payment is necessary. But if you do need assistance with the same issue later…a onetime extermination would cost about fifty to eighty thousand. And if you wanted the root of the problem dealt with, a multiple of that amount would cover it."

Had today's events been an actual quest, it would've fallen into the C or D rank.

"Hmm," the man hummed. He was staring thoughtfully into space.

"Wait a second… That means it would cost less than leaving

the issue as is and having to pay a premium for ordering blood oranges…?"

The man had already placed a consultation box in a corner of his establishment. Next to it, he'd even supplied a pen and paper.

"We'll come by every once in a while to check the box's contents and address the troubles."

"…Will Her Highness solve them like she did today?"

The man glanced at Maylee, who looked up at me questioningly.

"That will depend on the specifics of the job. There may be dangerous variables that we can't accept."

Nodding, the man replied, "Ah, of course."

Maylee pouted. "I can do it! Since I'm an adventurer, it won't be dangerous."

"Now, now," I said, stroking the girl's hair. Naturally, anyone who'd just completed their first battle felt invincible and on top of the world.

Maylee was at the level of an F ranker. Meaning, she couldn't normally tackle combat quests. I'd made an exception today because I'd been with her.

It seemed that we would be working on spreading the word of the eatery, Maylee, and the Adventurers Guild for a while. We would examine the requests in the consultation box, give people guidance at the guild, and do the initial quests pro bono.

I guess that's how it'll probably work.

I didn't have the power to decide on my own, so I'd need to talk it over with Iris later.

Bardenhawk's guild headquarters would gradually find its place so long as we used that system to spread the word.

I found Milia, Iris, and the others sightseeing around the capital and told them about the consultation box and how we would increase visibility.

"I see... That sounds like a great way of doing things. Everyone had these blank looks on their faces when we told them about adventurers, after all."

"Good idea, Mr. Roland! Without quests, a guild can't function anyhow."

And just like that, I had the go-ahead I needed.

The adventurers of the embarrassing Roland gang slowly began to trickle into the city.

◆

Several days passed without issue, and I was working at the guild. More and more adventurers I recognized had been stopping by.

"Boooosssss! Your favorite pupil, Neal, has arrived! I killed it!"

"I don't recall ever taking you on as a student. Also, please keep it down. You're bothering those around you."

"Guh, you're as cold as ever..."

"Boss, Neal is just happy. He's glad to help you," Roger, Neal's partner, said with a strained smile.

I explained to them what it meant to be a part of the broadscale quest.

"This is a special job," I told the pair. "Anyone who assists with establishing the new guild will be compensated in the end." Just as I had explained to the eatery owner, I told Neal and Roger we weren't a charity, and that money from the successful quests would become operating capital for the guild. "As the one responsible for this operation, I'll decide how we distribute funds and who we give them to. I will be watching you both closely, so please give it all you have."

"All riiight!" Neal was raring to go, while Roger told me they would be back again in a few days.

The pretty girl squad had also arrived while I'd been talking to the two men.

"Master Roland! We came as quickly as we could after hearing from the leader!" Eelu, who was now a proper mage in her own right, called out.

"The leader…you mean Neal?"

"Yes. He gathered everyone together. He looked so very grave when he told us you had something you needed from us, but he took so long to say it. It was a little annoying, but he made a funny expression," the beastperson Lyan said as her ears twitched.

"…It took so long getting here, but we did it for you, Master Roland." Sanz the dwarf had little to say, as always.

"As soon as the idea of paying you back was mentioned, they got so excited…" Su the elf looked over to the other three and shrugged.

"Don't listen to her, Master Roland. She was the most excited."

"Excuse me! That is irrelevant right now."

"Su always tries to act her best in front of you, Master Roland." *Nod nod.*

Chapter 4 111

"*Ahem...*" Su averted her eyes, seeming embarrassed.

The four girls had already made it to C rank and had accomplished all kinds of quests together. They would likely reach B rank soon.

Immediately after them, Geppetto, the boy with the shovel, made his way over. Although he'd initially failed the adventurer test, he'd later passed after seeing his skill in a new light.

"Sir! It's been too long!"

"It has indeed," I replied. "You've grown taller. And you've also gotten much more muscular."

The somewhat delicate mother's boy had entered a growth spurt.

Geppetto had a gigantic bundle on his back, and the handles of three different shovels were sticking out from it. He also carried a spear, which he hadn't had before.

We shared a solid handshake.

After rising to B rank, Geppetto had become a popular rookie.

"The construction guild kept asking me to come with them, and I've turned them down repeatedly, but once I heard that a certain guild worker was in trouble, I changed my mind."

"Thanks for pitching in. It seems you've become a splendid engineer in your own right. Did you learn how to use a spear as well?"

"Heh, yeah. Since I was so good at digging holes, I got invited into a ton of parties, and they taught me how to fight with polearms. Solo work's gotten easier, too. With my shovel, I can stay out in the woods or mountains for a long time and dig up ore, which is my strong suit. And it's all thanks to you."

"Not at all. These are the fruits of your own effort. You've come a long way from wildly brandishing a sword."

"Ah-ha-ha. Oh, c'mon, don't bring that up. I'd just gotten it into my head that all adventures involved combat. I feel like that happened ages ago."

"It hasn't even been a whole year yet," I replied.

"Wow, you're right," Geppetto said with a laugh.

That was just how packed his schedule had been since he'd become an adventurer.

"Miss Candey, Mr. Geppetto, and about half of the adventurers who've grown famous in their field seem to be part of the Roland gang," Milia muttered, as though she had come to a realization.

"They've amassed into quite a force," Iris remarked.

"It's true."

"Mm-hmm."

United force or not, as long as they kept that name, I'd never acknowledge their existence.

Later in the day, Maylee came by to spend time at the guild, and the two of us decided to check the eatery we'd visited before.

"How have things been? Did you get a lot?" I pointed at the consultation box, and the owner grinned.

"You should check and find out."

Maylee picked up the box and pulled off the lid.

"Wooow…! Roland! It's full!"

She showed it to me, and the box was indeed stuffed with

requests. The senders had even properly written their names and locations.

"It's only been a week," I said.

"I spread the word, and since people can apply for help with anything, submissions poured in."

"Evidently, they're starting to understand that there are people who can assist. I'm sure it'd be troublesome, but would you be able to send these to the Adventurers Guild in the future?" I asked.

"Yes, just leave that to me."

"Roland, am I going to do all of these?" Maylee inquired.

"We'll split them up among everyone."

Maylee was hopping about, so after getting her to settle down, we returned to the guild.

We'd fixed up the internal system we would be using to operate and had gathered quests and adventurers. Additionally, I'd copied the notes from the restaurant onto quest stubs and worked with several staff members to assign the quests ranks.

"Master Roland! What are you doing for lunch?" Eelu from the pretty girl squad had returned from some business. "I would be so happy if you could join us!"

"You came at just the right time," I told her.

"Oh, are you hungry? In that case…"

Handing Eelu four quest stubs, I said, "Could you divvy these up among the other three?"

"…Oh…you meant work. I see…" Eelu's shoulders drooped as she left the guild.

"Roland, what about my quests?!"

"You get this one, Maylee."

"'Take care of kids.' B-but…that's not an adventure!"

The young princess looked shocked and discouraged.

According to the job description, the eldest of the children was the same age as Maylee. The youngest was a baby, and there were four siblings in total. For an adult, a task like this was likely tougher than fighting. It would be easy for Maylee, however. All she would have to do was play with kids her age.

"Adventurers do more than battle. I'll even give you a partner."

I grabbed Rila, who had been curled up and sleeping at my feet.

"Oh, it's the black kitty that only eats, sleeps, and complains."

I handed Rila off to Maylee.

"*Nyah…?*"

Maylee hugged her tight.

"Gyaaaah?! That hurts! Gentler! Gentler!"

"Rila, you're gonna do a quest with me."

"Hmph? Well, I suppose I have no qualms. I *was* starting to grow bored."

Now that the black cat was going, another was sure to follow—Roje. She had been watching from outside this whole time and only now came inside.

"I have heard what is happening! If Lord Rileyla is venturing out, then I have no option but to accompany you as well. Let us be on our way, Maylee."

With Roje accompanying them, there was no need for a guard. I'd make Maylee, Roje, and the black cat work as a unit.

After that, I greeted the many familiar adventurers who arrived and arranged suitable quests for them.

The Bardenhawk Adventurers Guild was rapidly taking shape.

◆

"Rojey, we're planning to do an enemy-slaying quest today."

"Ah, but Maylee, you're still young and inexperienced. I doubt he would prepare a job like that for you…" Roje glanced at where I sat across the counter.

"Maylee, do not underestimate adventures," Rila cautioned from atop the princess's head. Then she laughed. According to Rila, Roje had been supporting Maylee and, though the elf did intervene at times, Maylee was handling most of the work.

"Hmm, are there any good slaying quests you can handle…?" I wondered aloud.

""You're surprisingly softhearted,"" Roje and Rila quipped.

Leyte had entrusted Maylee to me. Roje and Rila accompanied the girl, but I still couldn't let her get up to anything too reckless.

"Something has been attacking sheep and horses in a small pasture on the capital's outskirts. Your quest is to guard them."

Basically, it was just a lookout job.

"And then I fight off the baddies?" Maylee questioned eagerly.

I nodded. "That's right. If they come, that's what you'll do."

The work was for two days. If something happened during that time, Maylee and her two supervisors would be the first on the scene.

"You can leave it to me, Roland."

"Yes. I'm counting on you."

"Uh-huh!"

After giving me an enthusiastic response, Maylee departed with Roje and Rila in tow.

The harder Maylee worked at her quests, the more opportunities to spread awareness of the Adventurers Guild by word of mouth.

When I turned around, one of the Lahti branch staff members was pointing to the back of the office with his thumb. "Time for the shift change."

"Right, I suppose it is."

Earlier today, Iris and I had had a meeting with government officials at the castle. Now we had to report our progress to Leyte.

"Let's go, Roland."

"See you later." Milia saw us off with a nonchalant remark, and we set out along the winding, hilly road.

A familiar pair of guards let us in.

"Lady Leyte could have met with us when we were at the castle this morning to save us the round trip," Iris grumbled.

"She *is* the queen. I'm sure she's extremely busy," I responded.

"So that title isn't just for show, then. Sounds rather hectic…"

The staffers who had come with me had grown quite accustomed to castle life. They were no longer surprised and excited by the expensive meals that were served.

Iris and I headed into the conference room and took our seats. Immediately, two government officials we had already spoken with several times entered. One was thin in the face, and the other was slightly chubby. It seemed Leyte would be late, so we reported to them first.

After giving the officials the materials Iris and I had prepared the day before, I launched into an explanation.

I only told them about our daily operations, but I couldn't discern whether the men understood any of it. They had no comments.

"At the moment, these are our numbers, but the consultations are trending upward, and I believe that we should increase our staff size in response."

Iris and I were in agreement on his point.

The documents rustled as the chubbier man tossed the papers away.

"If we increase the number of staff, then where do their salaries come from? Are *we* supposed to pay for them?"

Iris was the one to reply. "Of course."

A frown formed on the chubby official's face. "You said you would handle everything, so we've permitted you to operate unrestricted."

The slender-faced man nodded in agreement.

"There was no mention of hiring more people and forcing us to pay the overhead."

"We can't say here forever. Training is necessary to install local people who will manage the guild properly. And the same applies to the adventurers."

At first, the two officials had been willing to listen, and we'd thought they would be easy to work with, but I realized that had been a misconception. They didn't care much about helping with our work. Whenever we checked in with them, they offered little feedback. Basically, they weren't very invested.

I'd observed that they only bothered to skip through the first page or two of documents Iris and I had provided.

"While you are state guests from Felind, some things are impermissible," the chubby man stated.

His and his associate's eyes all but said, *Why are you involving us in this?*

The two men were obviously disinterested, prompting Iris to say with frustration, "If you don't train staff to lay the groundwork, Felind Kingdom will be running your guild indefinitely!"

Iris and I had been working without a break since we'd arrived. Milia, considerate as she was, was working nonstop, too. However, that fact did little to move the pair of officials. Evidently, it meant nothing to them.

"Getting employees ready takes time, so you have to start as quickly as possible." I could see that Iris was becoming more agitated as she spoke.

I supposed these men didn't want to take responsibility for an odd-jobs system developed by another nation... Perhaps they'd thought the duty wouldn't involve any work. The pair of Bardenhawk government officials were in their seats, but they weren't at the table.

"Even if we permit you to hire more help...our country doesn't have the resources to create an appropriate budget," the chubby man argued.

"You likely haven't heard, but the queen declared that she's putting together a parliament, and the country is in the midst of chaos," added the thin-faced official.

They all but outright called us a nuisance and admitted they only attended the briefings because they had to.

"What are we supposed to report to the queen?"

"That this is taking more money? It's not as though she will look favorably on that. Even we have to tighten the purse strings as we allocate the budgets."

"As I said, the salaries—" Iris was on her feet now, and she appeared close to flying into a range, so I forced her to sit back down. "Ah! What do you think you're doing?!"

"You were scowling. It spoils your pretty face."

"Guh…"

Her irritation was reasonable, but that tone was ill-suited to negotiation. As she rubbed at the corners of her eyes next to me, I explained things in her stead.

"It won't require additional funds. The guild itself will generate the necessary revenue."

"Hmph. Easier said than done."

"That's right. How many people are you even planning to employ? Just think of how much it would cost to replace all of you Lahti workers…"

I flipped through the documents in my hands and thrust them at the officials.

"Here are the current projections for what we believe the guild will be making in one month, per quarter, and in half a year. It's all detailed in the papers you tossed away."

"'...Tsk.'"

The two of them read the forms I shoved in their faces.

"This is the amount after subtracting overhead. Right now, there are seven staff members on loan from Felind. Even if you have eleven people of your own, there will be enough profit to sustain them because the number of requests is still trending up."

Their whole spiel about not being able to do things because of money had likely been a facade. The more important officials were working on setting up the parliament.

"We are simply people sent from Felind, but you are the ones responsible for the guild. Do you understand?" Despite my words, they still looked like they didn't get it. "Consider this... If the guild is successful, then you two will take the credit. Felind helped, but your names are the ones that will be associated with this project down the line."

That elicited a reaction from them. All this pair cared about was themselves. After realizing that, I decided to press my attack.

Sighing, I said, "It's too bad. I suppose the only thing to do is talk to Queen Leyte about changing the leadership on the project."

"N-now just wait there."

"Y-yes. There's no need to be so hasty..."

Iris shrugged as though she had given up.

"Then will you work with us?" I asked.

"'Of course,'" the officials agreed with eager expressions.

It was like night and day compared to the start of the meeting. Iris and I exchanged strained smiles.

"These are some nice materials."

"All we did was put together the objective numbers."

"It really helps to have such competent people."

"With this, we should be able to rest a bit."

"Right."

Iris and I shared a high five under the table.

It seemed Bardenhawk was home to many people who didn't like taking ownership over their work. Fortunately, now that the officials were motivated, they acted on our proposal to recruit more staff. There were nearly twenty applications for two openings a week later.

If we accepted a lot of people at the start, things would get out of hand, so we decided the best course was to train only a few at first, then recruit more later.

"You could do it, Roland, but you can pretty much do anything, right? So I'd like you to handle the normal work rather than teaching the new people."

According to Iris, Milia was overseeing the recent hires.

Though the guild management was busy, everything proceeded smoothly.

"What are you here for today?"

A man who looked somewhat like an adventurer, but wasn't one of the ones I recognized, had come by. I asked him for his guild card.

He was an A-rank adventurer. That confused me, as I wasn't aware of any adventurers in the Roland gang at that level other than Dey.

"I'm from Bardenhawk originally," he explained. "I heard about the guild being set up here."

"I see. So that's what brought you here."

"After the demon lord's army destroyed the duchy, I thought I'd never step foot in my homeland again… Now they're rebuilding, and I want to help."

"You're here to aid your homeland? Truthfully, we don't have many high-ranking adventurers like you, and it's given us a bit of trouble. Your assistance is most welcome."

"Thank you, sir!"

Behind the man, I saw three other members of his party.

They were all born in Bardenhawk and had come with the A ranker.

"I'm afraid we won't be able to offer the type of payment that you would receive at a Felind Adventurers Guild…," I told them. Then I presented three vanquishing quest stubs to the group.

One was for dispatching a formidable monster, the next was a tricky magical beast, and the third a swarm of creatures. Each job was A rank.

The rewards were about one-third of what they would've been in Felind. I'd done the on-scene investigation for these quests myself, so I explained what to look out for to the men.

The A-rank adventurer seemed unfazed.

"Payment shouldn't be an issue. Right, guys? You're good with this?"

"Yes. Actually, the reward seems on the higher side to me."

"Are you an idiot? It's cheap. But, well, we didn't come here for the money."

"I agree. If we were after riches, we wouldn't have spent a week traveling here."

Each gave his opinion in turn.

"...So there you have it. Please leave these to us, sir."

"Thank you. I look forward to your results," I said.

"You're not from the capital, are you, sir?" one of the men asked me.

"I'm not," I replied. "I normally work at the Lahti branch."

"That explains it."

The whole party nodded, looking satisfied.

"You're very courteous, sir."

"This is how I normally conduct myself," I replied.

"We'll be in hot water if we screwed up after all the info you gave us. It'd call our ranks into question."

"Ha-ha-ha. I suppose so," laughed the A-rank adventurer, while I was stuck for a response. "At any rate, I've fought off these types of foes multiple times, so I'm sure we'll do fine. You know, if you worked in Finlan, I'm sure you'd become a mighty popular guild worker."

"Oh, I'm not so sure about that," I said.

"If you ever were assigned there, I'd come in to work with you."

The A-rank adventurer chuckled and nodded before leaving with his companions.

I'd always thought adventurers only made decisions based on the work involved in a quest and the payout. Since they risked their lives for the job, that seemed obvious. Until today, I'd never thought men like this A ranker existed. They were something like warriors of loyalty and patriotism.

"How ironic. Anyone can be an adventurer, yet they're more chivalrous than actual knights."

I hoped they would come home safely.

As I filed their quest acceptances, I heard a hoarse voice call, "Bosssss!"

Neal had hurried over noisily and was now sitting across from me.

Without taking my eyes off the documents, I asked, "Is this about earlier?"

"Yes, there was this fortune-teller with Clairvoyance or whatever. I thought they might fit what you're looking for."

"Mm-hmm. Clairvoyance…"

Some idiot with a skill of the same name had once blackmailed me. I wondered whether it was the same skill.

"I've been looking for them all over Izaria this whole week, and I think this person's the closest one we've got. There's been no word of anyone else possessing something like Appraisal or Skill Detection."

The guild was looking for people with special skills that would allow them to see others' skills. I'd asked Neal to gather information for me.

"Is that right? Thank you very much," I replied.

"We really do need someone… It takes time sending every single person to Felind just to meet with someone who has Appraisal."

Chapter 4

"Yes. And even if they take the adventurer exam, if we don't know what skill they have, it'll be difficult to judge them."

Unfortunately, Bardenhawk didn't have a tradition of people finding out what their skills were.

About half of the populace used their abilities without realizing what they were doing. The other half weren't using them and were just in the dark.

This had kept me from finding any with the Appraisal or Skill Detection skills.

Knowing your own skill made a huge impact in battle.

Supposedly, skills developed around the age of ten, and since the people of Felind and Bardenhawk were not much different, the same would probably hold true for the people of this country.

"Could you tell me where this fortune-teller is? I will go see them myself," I said.

"Then, if I may be so bold, I, Neal, would like to accompany you…"

"No, please do more quests. We have plenty of low-rank ones."

"…Okay."

I took the note Neal had hastily jotted down.

No adventurers or applicants were waiting, so I told Iris I was going out, and I left the guild.

The location Neal had written down wasn't far; it was still within the capital's walls.

In the poorer sections, there were many deserted houses whose only visitors were the occasional thief. The scars of war remained in the form of burned-down dwellings left to rot.

I stopped in front of an old single-story home and knocked three times on its door.

If Neal's information was right, then a fortune-teller by the name of Betty lived here.

"Hello. Is Ms. Betty in?" I called.

I heard the sound of footsteps. A moment later, the door flew open.

"Whatcha want? Comin' here in the early morning..." A woman still in her undergarments stood in the entrance. Although she couldn't have been as old as thirty, she was rather inarticulate and smelled of booze.

"It's past noon," I told her. "Are you Ms. Betty?"

"Ngh? What's it to you if I am? ...Huh?!"

When she saw me, Betty opened her eyes wide and slammed the door shut.

"Um? Are you okay?"

"I-I'm not... A man?! But I'm practically undressed..."

"It's all right. I paid no mind to it at all, and it didn't bother me."

"Well, that's hurtful in a different way... Actually, it's kinda rude."

"I'd like for you to tell me my fortune."

"...Oh, so you're a customer..."

I heard some whispers, then a commotion, then silence.

"All right. Come right in."

At her invitation, I entered.

The place was old and small. It was basically a one-room abode. The corners of the room were filled with liquor bottles.

Betty was standing prim and proper—and fully clothed.

"I-I don't have a place for you to sit, so please take the bed..."

Chapter 4   127

"Thank you."

As I sat down, the frame creaked ominously.

Betty was playing with her hair, twisting it around while refusing to meet my gaze.

"I heard you're able to tell fortunes," I commented.

"Yeah… Y-yes…I can. For twenty thousand. I'll do it for twenty thousand hawks."

"I'm sorry. All I have are rins."

"Then that'll do."

There were many types of fortunes. There was even a chance that her reading would reveal nothing related to skills.

I retrieved two paper bills from my wallet and placed them on the table. Upon seeing her payment, Betty immediately got to work.

"I have an interesting power… You could call it an ability, I suppose. I just used it, and I can tell what you are…"

If she knew who I was, then there was no point in feigning anymore.

"Does your 'ability' tell you what skill I have?" I inquired.

"What a miserable power you have…," Betty replied with a sniffle. She wiped the corners of her eyes with her hands.

"Enough to cry over?" I asked.

The woman nodded readily.

"Since there's no real way to use it?"

"No. That's not what I mean," she clarified. "That's not what I'm saying at all. I can see memories of your skill…of the tremendous amount of time and effort you put into it. I'm also aware of your various 'exploits.'"

"...I'd be grateful if you could keep those to yourself."

"Of course. I don't tell others about my clients. Knowing who you are, I'd be in serious trouble if I did."

"That's right," I answered.

We spent some time in silence until Betty spoke again.

"It looks like your skill was stolen once."

"What? It was?"

"Oh, did I get that wrong?"

"I don't think anything like that's happened..."

"I see. Then please just ignore that. Anyway, I've divined that your power makes it difficult for others to notice you."

"..."

It had been stolen? Betty had to be mistaken. That bothered me, but if she could tell this much, that was more than enough.

"Adventurer hopefuls will occasionally come your way. When they do, would you please use your ability to determine their skills and tell them what they are?" I requested.

"So long as they're willing to pay..."

"Naturally, you will be compensated."

"Then sure."

"I've given up assassination. I'm sorry if I scared you," I told her.

Betty shook her head. "I saw how many you killed and saved, so please don't worry about it."

"I've asked you for something without bringing a gift in return. I'll bring you liquor next time."

Chapter 4

"You don't have to. But since you offered, make sure it's something good," Betty replied. "You're welcome anytime."

She laughed quietly.

I felt like she would get along with Rila.

Before leaving, I said, "You can count on it."

5
Starting with Collection Quests A to Z, Part I

We had no end of *konsou*-gathering E-rank quests. As soon as a few were completed, more came in to take their places. No matter how many we assigned to the low-rank adventurers, the number would not go down. It felt as though E-rank quests were the only type we were arranging.

"We never run out of this quest…," I commented to no one in particular, but Milia, who had become the trainee instructor, responded, "Oh, lots of places have been ordering *konsou*-gathering quests…"

Many of them were commission jobs that gave an increased payout the more you gathered.

Konsou was a type of medicinal herb used for healing potions, so the clients were apothecaries, secondhand shops, and, occasionally, researchers.

In Bardenhawk, which was still rebuilding, there weren't enough materials to go around. Water and food were limited, but medical supplies in particular were hard to come by.

Maylee was off with Roje and cat-form Rila on an F-rank quest today. I was happy they were all enjoying themselves.

As I was taking care of some office work, the pretty girl squad arrived. They'd taken one of the *konsou*-gathering quests earlier.

"Master Roland, we're back."

The leader, Eelu, sat across from me to make her report.

"Thank you for your work. How did it go?" I inquired.

Lyan, the beastperson, set a bag on the counter. The contents only barely filled my hands.

"This was all we could manage, Master Roland...," she said dejectedly. I gave her a pat on the head.

"Don't be too down. I'm sure this will be a great help. This is the most that anyone has collected recently."

"...It is?" Sanz the dwarf questioned in her hushed voice.

"Yes. I looked into some of the quest submissions, and the demand hasn't increased, but the supply is low. Herbs are scarce, it seems," I explained.

Su the elf said, "We searched spots where *konsou* was likely to grow, but we mostly found traces of plants that had already been harvested."

I flipped through the collection of E-rank quests.

"There are some clients who submit a new request immediately after they obtain a certain amount. Others keep the quest open indefinitely because they never get enough product no matter how much is delivered."

"Lyan and Su know the woods well, so we don't have trouble finding new spots where *konsou* is growing, but...even when we locate it, there's so little," Eelu stated, and the other three girls nodded.

According to them, there'd hardly been anything nearby, forcing them to search farther from the capital.

"If we don't have healing potions, lots of people will be in trouble...," I remarked.

Eelu and the others wore obviously thoughtful and troubled expressions.

Since they'd completed their task, I arranged another quest for them and sent the group off.

"Is *konsou* getting scarce?" Milia asked softly. It seemed she'd been listening.

Nodding, I answered, "It seems so."

Healing potions were essential to adventurers and normal people alike. If this continued, there'd be fewer potions to go around, and people would start hoarding. That, in turn, would drive prices up, keeping the valuable items out of the hands of those who needed them.

In order to learn more about the shortage, I walked over to a medicine shop in Izaria.

I asked how scarce healing potions were; how much they would need to have enough; and how much *konsou* that would require.

"...I've been searching high and low myself, but there really isn't any *konsou* to find," the apothecary explained. "It almost makes me suspect someone has been snatching it all up," he added with a laugh. "I did see a lot of tsunorabi while I was looking, though."

"Tsunorabi...? As in the horned rabbits?"

"Yes. There seem to be a lot of them around."

"They are omnivorous, after all."

"Right. Which is why I suspect they've been eating all the *konsou*."

It didn't seem like such an odd thought, but they were unlikely to only eat the *konsou*.

I thanked the shopkeeper and left.

I went to look at a nearby meadow before heading back to the guild, then consulted with Iris.

"Hmm... In that case, should we try to figure out what to do about the tsunorabi first?"

"They aren't eating up all *konsou* specifically. I think it's more that there's been a population boom, and they're eating all kinds of plants."

"So anything they consider food will become scarce, including *konsou*."

"Tsunorabi meat can be made into jerky. If the guild offers to buy them, we can put out extermination quests," I suggested.

"That's perfect! What a great idea! Let's do that now."

Iris went right along with my proposal.

"What a lot of trouble this has been... *Konsou* quests kept coming in, and I'm sure you had to assign them to adventurers who normally would've been given different jobs, right?"

I nodded. Iris seemed to understand the situation well.

"It's caused a delay for other quests," I noted.

"I'm sure there are mid- and upper-level adventurers who like hunting, so they'll likely help out with the tsunorabi."

Unfortunately, culling them wouldn't bring back the *konsou* immediately, but it was the first step.

We immediately started up a horned-rabbit–hunting quest and began taking applicants that day.

"Boss, looks like it's time for me to really go all out…!"

Neal, whose preferred weapon was a bow, looked fired up, despite the quest being E rank.

"I feel bad for the bunnies, but…you've deemed this a serious affair! I'll do all in my power as well." Roger also appeared sufficiently motivated.

"The guild will pay one thousand rins per rabbit. Please make sure to drain the blood from any you kill. If you're unable to do so, bring it in alive," I said.

""Yes, sir!""

No sooner did the pair of men leave than the pretty girl squad entered.

"A-are we hunting bunnies?" Eelu asked with a scowl.

"Master Roland…I like tsunorabi and seeing them around… Can't we keep them as pets?"

"You can, but we can't give you a reward."

"…But tsunorabi are so cute…"

Lyan and Sanz also seemed disappointed by the development.

In contrast, Su said indifferently, "Weren't you listening to Master Roland? Things could get rough if we don't have healing potions."

Their party had no healer, so potions were essential. Without them, the girls wouldn't be able to go on adventures. A shortage could mean a spike in adventurer deaths, too.

Su checked her bowstring as she spoke. "One for a thousand rins. Between Lyan and me, we should be able to get twenty, no problem."

"Master Roland, I like money, so I'll work my hardest," Eelu declared, her eyes glistening. Lyan and Sanz agreed.

"I'm counting on you all," I told them.

After that, I arranged the horned-rabbit–hunting quest for other adventurers I recognized.

"If you're the one asking me, Mr. Roland, I can't say no…"

"I…would kill anything for your sake, Master Roland…anyone, too…"

"This isn't the time for dillydallying! I'll show you what I can do and make sure I'm girlfriend-candidate material…!"

Evidently, the women were highly motivated.

"I-if I hunt more than anyone else, please go to a restaurant with me!" one of them shouted as she turned red and waited for me to answer, while everyone else held their breath.

"All right. If you can do that, I'll thank you by treating you to a meal."

""""It's like a dream come true!""""

Suddenly, the women got competitive, and they began to act somewhat bloodthirsty.

"I'll kill those rabbits."

"Kill, kill, kill."

"Kill a ton of them."

"Kill more than anyone else!"

The ladies departed, a dark aura emanating from them.

There was something bothering me, so I talked to Iris about the situation and got her permission to leave the guild.

I left Izaria on horseback and rode to the woods to take a look around. It didn't take long to confirm my suspicions.

"They don't have natural predators."

That was why the creatures were multiplying.

All of the footprints in the mulch were small. None had come from predators or large monsters. I saw several other sets of tracks, but the situation was the same each time.

According to the guild staff manual, there were certain magical beasts, monsters, and animals that were not to be hunted. They included harmless magical beasts and species of animals that were in decline and nearing endangerment.

At a spot deep in the woods and far from the capital, I spotted a magical beast from afar—a gray wolf.

They had grown to avoid humans, for they knew that getting near any was dangerous. Thus, they also rarely attacked people. They had been hunted to near extinction long ago, and now killing them was forbidden worldwide.

However, that only applied to humans. Other things threatened the wild creatures.

"...I didn't see any in other spots around the forest."

Gray wolves preyed on tsunorabi. If they were scarce, it followed that the tsunorabi population would increase.

That had to mean someone was killing gray wolves.

As I was watching the magical beast, I sensed someone.

"..."

I listened for footsteps until I spotted an unshaven man setting up a large trap. I could tell immediately it wasn't meant to catch smaller animals.

"Hey. Are you the one hunting the gray wolves?"

"Huh?! What? Who the hell are you?"

"Hunting gray wolves is prohibited. Your actions are causing a healing potion shortage."

"Hah. Why should I care?"

"I see." I sped forward and thrust a small twig from the ground near his eye. "Then I suppose if you were to become the gray wolf's meal, no one else would care?"

"Wh-wh-who are you!"

"I'm sure a gray wolf pelt fetches a high price. You were poaching them to sell, right?"

"Uh."

"Seems I hit the bull's-eye. Now tell me what you know. You came all the way out here into the woods to set up traps, so you must be a lackey."

"Hah! Why would I tell you anything?"

"You have two eyes. Losing one wouldn't blind you, at the very least."

I slowly brought the twig that I held in a backhanded grip closer to his face, and he began to sweat.

"St-stop... Stop..."

"Do you feel like talking now?"

The man held both his hands up in surrender.

"I-I'll tell you everything! S-so please! No more! I'm sorry…"

The man told me he was part of the Welger Company.

I hadn't heard that name before. Depending on the region, certain companies were known as merchant guilds. Lots of traders sought membership in those groups.

However, this man didn't look like some peddler to me.

"We deal in everything. You can trade in whatever you like, and we procure products based on demand," he explained.

That sounded like a poaching-and-smuggling ring, but the organization likely hid behind a kinder public front.

"I see. So right now, gray wolf pelts are highly sought-after," I said.

"Y-yes…"

Since I'd been holding the twig up to his eye this whole time, the man's voice was quavering.

While hunting certain beasts was illegal, the sale of products derived from them wasn't.

It was strange to think about, but humans were the one thing that was plentiful in this world.

"Apparently, gray wolf pelts are a status symbol in some country. We've been making a killing selling them to the rich folks over there."

"I'd like you to explain this all in detail in the knights' guardroom."

It wasn't my job to deal with criminals.

"Sure…but you should know that the Welger Company doesn't abandon its people. They'll come for me."

Chapter 5   139

"Are you sure they'd be so quick to rescue a man who outed their dealings?"

"Well, look, they don't know that."

The man was wilier than I thought. Apprehending an underling like him didn't solve anything. At this rate, the gray wolves would disappear. Then the forests would become a paradise for smaller animals, and medicinal plants like *konsou* would be all but impossible to get.

That would spell trouble for adventurers and the guild. Ordinary citizens would surely suffer from the lack of medicines, too.

"It would be a terrible chain reaction."

I couldn't let that happen.

"Would they retaliate and rescue you from any Order of Chivalry outpost I drop you off at? No matter the town?"

"Naturally."

All right. So what's the quickest and most logical way to deal with this...

"..."

I put down the twig and tried to reason with the man by pretending to drop my hostility.

"In that case, there's no reason for me to capture you," I said.

"R-really?!"

"In exchange, I want in on the action. I'll ask adventurers where to find gray wolves and leak the info to you."

"Heh-heh-heh. Guess you're not all that pure either, huh?"

"I'm not a bad guy. All I'm doing is having a lighthearted conversation with you, an acquaintance, about work without the faintest idea of what's going on."

"In the case, how's fifty thousand rins per wolf sound?"

That was a rather hefty sum indeed.

Someone was undoubtedly skimming from the top, which meant the fifty thousand was a share of the proceeds after that.

"...All right."

"Still, we're dealing with wild magical beasts here. Even if I use your info and set traps, I might not catch anything. And remember, you're just a guy I happen to know who offers me some useful tips without any knowledge of what I'm doing."

"That's right."

I had no idea who was using the pelts, but this Welger Company *was* smuggling them. The goods undoubtedly crossed many hands. I had to wonder how much the wolves actually went for.

Since it seemed the buyers were affluent, they were likely nobles.

"There's a forest that few adventurers explore," I said. "Have you gone there yet?"

"Oh? Where? You'd be doing me a favor by telling me."

"Since few adventurers go there, there are a lot of gray wolves around. I haven't checked for myself how many, but there's likely more than you'd find here."

I explained the location to the man while walking and leading my horse by its reins.

"I knew I could count on you, guild worker! You'll be a reliable source."

"That's just what I know off the top of my head. You should bring over some members of your company. That forest is dangerous enough that adventurers won't touch the place, after all."

"You're right. One or two people wouldn't be enough."

"Let me know what day you're going. I can show you the most efficient spots to set up the traps."

"That will be of great help." After a "see ya," the man clapped me on the shoulder and departed. He was awfully gullible.

I headed back to the guild to report.

"The gray wolf population in the woods has diminished."

I also told Iris how that related to the increasing number of tsunorabi. However, I kept the part about the Welger Company from her. I wanted to look into that later on my own. If I told her, there was a chance she might be drawn into the group's machinations.

"What's to be done about this?" Iris tapped on her desk with her fingertips.

"I can investigate the cause and eliminate the problem," I offered.

"Hmm, I feel like this doesn't fall under staff work…but this *is* an issue of life and death for adventurers," Iris replied. "All right, you can handle it."

"Okay."

Not knowing when my opportunity to strike would arise, I decided to make some preparations.

◆

Three days had passed.

On the way to the guild, I came across the unshaven man. As we passed by each other, we spoke in hushed tones.

"Today. Woods at noon."

"Got it."

"We're counting on you."

Since we hadn't even looked at one another, anyone who'd seen us surely thought we'd simply passed right by without saying a word.

...*I wonder how many pests will show up.*

After the morning assembly was over, I headed to the manager's office and explained the situation.

Once I had permission to leave, I finished my work before noon and hurried to the forest by horse.

A group of men dressed like ruffians was waiting at the edge of the woods. Many of them clearly had combat experience. All told, there were around fifty of them, which made this seem like a large-scale military operation.

"Hey, over here!" the unshaven man called with his hand raised.

"Looks like you've gathered everyone," I remarked.

"'Course I have."

Apparently, the others were members of the Welger Company, too, but they typically operated in other regions.

With just a glance, I could tell they weren't excited about the hunt, and they didn't seem scared by the gray wolves. I got the impression they were seasoned in this.

Among the people, one man had a different air about him. He was young and muscular.

"This is Mr. Bale. He's in charge of the merchandise."

Once I was introduced, I invoked my magic and shook hands with Bale.

Chapter 5

He'd just shaken hands with someone he hadn't met before without a care in the world. It didn't seem like he had any self-preservation instincts. Perhaps he left himself defenseless because he expected always to be the predator and not the prey.

"You've done quite a lot for my people," he said.

"It's a give-and-take relationship," I replied.

"...What was that magic you used?"

"It's a type of spell to make one less noticeable."

"Hmm. You seem quite knowledgeable."

"Well, these woods are plentiful, so the gray wolves here grow strong."

As I inspected the equipment of the gathered men, I cast spells on them. Roje had taught me this particular magic the other day.

"All right, that's enough for introductions. We've gotta set up all these traps before the sun sets."

Little did they know they were the ones walking into a snare. I could have killed them all where they stood, but it would take time and effort to get rid of the bodies. Plus, if they fled in different directions, there was a chance I'd miss a few.

Thus, it was most effective if they suffered unfortunate accidents in the woods.

We broke off into groups and went their separate ways into the woods. I was part of the same group as the unshaven man and Bale.

"You never know what could happen in a forest at night, so we always place the traps while the sun's up," the unshaven man explained.

After ten minutes, the magic started to work.

Howls and battle cries erupted from all around us.

""""Gaahhhhhhhh?!"""""

Shrieks of death echoed through the trees.

"Didja hear a scream just now?"

"Yes, I did..."

The rest of the group went on guard. And no sooner had they done so than four gray wolves appeared.

"Tsk, s-so they've come out to play, huh."

"Calm down. They're not predisposed to attack human—"

""""Awooooo!"""""

The gray wolves looked pretty bloodthirsty. Their eyes were entirely different from any beast's I'd seen before.

"Hmm. The magic seems pretty effective," I remarked.

Someone grabbed me violently by the shoulder.

"Hey! What'd you do?!"

"You're the ones who attacked them first," I said.

"What're you talking about?!"

The gray wolves were charging for us now. Each was a different size, but they were all as big as large dogs.

"Careful not to get bit. Their fangs can easily crush a human skull," I cautioned mockingly.

"What—what did you do?!" Bale grabbed me by the shirt collar.

"I actually placed a spell called Hater on you. Elves use it when hunting to find monsters more easily. During the war, they'd use it on the largest and sturdiest of their people who stood at the vanguard."

A wolf had torn right into the arm of a spear-wielding man, causing him to shriek.

Chapter 5

"The effect makes you a more desirable target. Everyone except for me has had Hater placed on them."

"Awoooo!"

A gray wolf leaped and clamped down on the unshaven man's neck.

"Ah! Ghhk...?!"

With a shake of its head, the beast sent the man's head flying from his body.

"You tricked us! You bastard!"

"What gave you the idea that I wouldn't? Aren't you the ones always deceiving others?"

Bale brandished his sword, hoping to keep the enraged creatures from reaching him.

"How does it feel to fall for a trap and be hunted?"

One of our group had been eaten, another was missing a leg, and a third had had his throat torn out. Bale was the last man standing.

Cries sounded from every direction as people met their grisly ends. The woods were pandemonium.

Apparently, Hater didn't last long, and once the spell was broken, the gray wolves would return to their usual business. This was also my first time using it, so I hadn't known how well it would work until I saw for myself. As a backup, I'd stationed a very frightening vampire nearby.

She was undoubtedly going around and putting the men out of their misery. I'd also given her one other job, which she'd been only too happy to accept.

"Why did you do this?" Bale demanded.

"A lesser evil will always be destroyed by a greater evil. That's all this is."

Bale turned his back on me and fled. The gray wolves tried to follow, but I released my murderous presence upon them. The beasts, mouths dripping crimson, quivered with fear. After a fleeting glance at me, they ran off in the opposite direction.

All that remained was to await a report from Dey.

"I'm sure she'll do a good job of it."

Though her kind were known for operating well at night, they were also specialists at dealing with the opposite sex.

◆Bale◆

Once Bale made it out of the woods, he kept running as fast as he could, even as his knees started to give way. A gray wolf had raked his back, but he had managed to escape in one piece, which was more than could be said for his associates. He felt a growing chill, possibly due to blood loss, and he was panting loudly.

The faces of the terrifying, bloodthirsty beasts dominated his thoughts, and so he quickly lost his way.

Eventually, he only saw the ground, and he realized he'd fallen over. Fear seized Bale as he recognized he was to perish like all the rest.

"Oh dear, oh dear. Oh my, oh my. You're so bloody... Your

death would be so troublesome... I wonder, are you still alive? Hello? Helllooo?"

Right before Bale lost consciousness, he saw the face of a beautiful woman for just a moment.

She was there by his side when he woke. She told him her name was Candey.

"As in...like *candy*?"

"Preeetty much. Won't you tell me your name?"

The woman who spoke a little oddly watched Bale from beside the bed.

"I'm Bale, twenty-six."

"I see." Candey smiled. "You were bloody when I found you on the ground, so I brought you all the way over here. Oh...and this is the inn I'm staying at."

Candey told Bale what had happened since he had lost consciousness. She had used some healing potion and saved his life. He'd been asleep for three days.

Just recalling what had transpired nearly caused Bale to wet himself with fear.

He'd heard the screams of his comrades in the woods, the sounds of their death wails, the howling of the wolves...

The claw marks on his back throbbed in pain.

"Did some monster get youuu?"

"Yeah... Normally they're docile...but they were different that day..."

"You can't underestimate themmm. Monsters are monsters, and people are people. We live our lives differently."

"It's not like I planned to get in a fight..."

"You're not an adventurer, then...?"

"An...adventurer?"

"Oh, right, lots of people here don't know what those are." The woman giggled, captivating Bale's attention.

She told him about everything as she fed him a healing potion.

It seemed she had made her way here from a kingdom called Felind to the northwest.

"I've become an adventurer and take on quests to make money."

"...But you're so pretty. Why would you do anything that dangerous...?"

"Oh myyy, don't flatter me. That won't work on me, Bale."

"That wasn't what I meant..."

She was oddly charming. There was something graceful about her expressions, the structure of her face, and even how her eyes moved. Bale had initially believed her to be the daughter of an aristocrat. She easily eclipsed all other women he knew.

Bale's mouth was dry, and he felt his heart quicken. When their eyes met, he quickly averted his eyes, and his face flushed.

"All right. Now it's your turn, Bale. What were you doing, and how did you end up like that? Won't you tell me?"

Suddenly, he felt something cold behind Candey's smile.

If he told her about himself, he wouldn't be able to avoid talking about the Welger Company. That wasn't something he could reveal to others.

"...Who cares about me? It's not a fun story."

Bale balled his hands into fists. He was surprised when Candey

Chapter 5   149

placed her soft, delicate hands on his. No, it was how cold they were that truly astonished him.

If he didn't tell Candey anything, there was a possibility he would never see her again.

"I want to know more about you…"

Her sweet voice made his mind go numb.

◆Roland◆

After dealing with the wolf-hunters, who all seemed to be low-rank flunkies for the Welger Company, I headed back to the guild and reported to Iris.

"I found people hunting gray wolves, but I dealt with them. The population should recover and help keep the tsunorabi under control."

"Thank you. The tsunorabi-hunting quests are going well, too, so we should have more *konsou* before long. I think a thousand rins per rabbit might have been a bit high, but if we make jerky and sell it, we should be all right." Iris looked at the notebook open on her desk and nodded.

"There's not enough cattle or pigs for food right now," I said. "People might be excited to have rabbit."

"I suppose," Iris replied, then a smirk formed on her face as though she had recalled something. "Roland, the princess was looking for you. She was in tears."

"…In tears?"

"She was begging us not to kill the bunnies."

"I see. I'll take the fall for this one."

"Please do. I think you're the only one who can."

I bowed, then left Iris's office.

In the main room, I found the adventurers waiting their turn with their tsunorabi. Some had caught them alive and, in an apparent misunderstanding, one had allowed theirs to get free in the guild, which was creating quite the commotion.

"Over there! It went over there! Please catch it!"

Milia was making a big deal of it as she and the adventurer scrambled around trying to catch the tsunorabi together.

It was a spectacle.

Once I reached my seat, I felt eyes on me. I searched for one watching and found a teary-eyed Maylee with Rila in her arms.

Roje was behind her.

With a look, I asked if the two adults had explained things to her, but they turned away.

I was sure they understood the situation.

"Roland…!" Maylee called.

"Is something the matter?" I asked her.

"Why are you killing the bunnies? The poor bunnies…"

"Maylee, you're still an F-rank adventurer, so you're not eligible for the E-rank tsunorabi-hunting quests yet. Don't worry, you won't have to hurt them," I tried to redirect the conversation, but it was to no avail.

"But they're soft, fluffy, and warm! Why are you hurting them?!"

Maylee was trying to hold back her sobs. She gave Rila a tight squeeze.

"Ngyaaaah?! Y-you're crushing me!"

"Maylee, stop that. You will squash Lord Rileyla."

The princess's eyes were red and her throat quivered as she set her mouth into a thin frown.

"Look, Maylee, what would you do if Leyte were injured?" I questioned.

"If Mother were…? I would help her…"

"And you would use medicine to do it, yes?"

"Yeah…"

"But the bunnies are eating the ingredient we use for medicine, and we don't have enough to go around. There are people in trouble."

"Is Mother…is Mother going to die…?"

The sadness she'd been holding back suddenly came pouring out in full force.

"I don't want her to die… I don't…*hic*… Uh… wahhhhhhhhhhh!"

Rila and Roje flew into action when they saw Maylee sobbing.

"Maylee, calm down. Leyte isn't dying. She shall not perish. He was speaking hypothetically!"

"Th-that's right, Maylee. Wh-why don't we go out for some ice cream after this? It's cold and sweet."

"I don't wannaaaaa!"

Unable to stand it, Rila leaped behind the counter to hide. "M-my ears…"

Roje glared at me. "Really now. This only happened because of your unnecessary example."

"Don't give me that when you didn't explain a thing to her so that she wouldn't be upset with you."

"You're stupid, Rolaaaand!" Maylee cried through her sobbing.

The adventurers in the office looked over, trying to figure out what was going on.

"Oh! The bunny is headed towards Mr. Roland! M-Mr. Roland!" Milia called out to me as the tsunorabi attempted to slip past my feet.

I grabbed it by the neck just as it entered my range. The creature kicked its legs in an attempt to escape from my grip.

"Oh, a bunny..." Maylee's waterworks immediately dried up.

"...Would you like to take it home? If you do, we won't hurt this one."

"Uh-huh... I'll take it..."

I'll have to explain this to Leyte later...

I handed the adventurer who had brought in the tsunorabi a thousand rins.

Maylee stared at the rabbit, so I asked her, "Want to hold it?" She gave me an enthusiastic nod.

"Be careful of the little horn. And watch out if it struggles."

"Okay."

Maylee sniffled loudly as she gently received the tsunorabi. Luckily, the monster obediently allowed itself to be held by Maylee.

"It's warm...and soft and fluffy... You're so cute, bunny..."

Chapter 5

A voice at my feet asked, "Knave, why have you given me a rival?"

"Don't give me that when all you do is try to curry her favor."

"Hmph. Just now, when I glared at it, it glared back at me! I am the demon lord, you know. I shall show you who ranks higher."

Maylee would likely give more attention to the tsunorabi than Rila for a while.

"Come to think of it, knave, I still have seen no sign of Dey. Is she on a quest?"

Rila and her guard, Roje, had been accompanying Maylee on her adventures. Dey didn't always go with them, but she saw them once every day at the very least.

"Dey is on a long-term quest. She…won't be back for a while."

Roje looked puzzled.

"A long-term quest? Did this country have such tasks?"

"Roje Sandsong, the Hater spell you taught me was very helpful. Thank you."

"Ngh?! I-I feel uncomfortable just hearing you thank me…"

"Should I say it again?"

"No! Stop it!!"

While Maylee was taken with her new pet, a group of knights and Luno, the lady-in-waiting we often saw, came to retrieve her.

Once she'd completed her work, the princess always waited at the guild for them to pick her up. Since they would always come at the same time, Rila and Roje would wait with her to say good-bye when the time came.

"Oh, Lady Alias. Where did that bunny come from?" Luno inquired. Maylee held the tsunorabi under its forelegs and thrust it forward.

"I'm taking it home!" she proclaimed.

"Is that right? I thought you wanted a cat…"

Maylee shook her head. "Not anymore!"

"*Hiss!*" Rila seemed to be in shock. As the tsunorabi left, she said begrudgingly to it, "Damn you, Bunnyton!"

◆

I headed to the castle with Maylee, the knights, and Luno.

"Are you going to convince Mother to let me keep it, Roland?" Maylee looked up at me as she cradled the tsunorabi.

"Convince her? I doubt Leyte would mind a single tsunorabi…"

She doted upon Maylee. The girl was her daughter, not to mention her last remaining family member.

However, Luno shook her head.

"Her Majesty does not spoil Lady Alias, Master Roland."

"Is that right?"

We headed down the long corridor, past the spacious hall that was the throne room, until we were finally standing before Leyte's personal chambers.

Maylee knocked, told her what we were here for, then she answered through the door, "Take it back. You cannot toy with a life so lightly."

Chapter 5

Maylee's face clouded over at her parent's strict words. She turned to look at me. I supposed this meant it was my turn.

"Lady Leyte, it's Roland."

"Oh, so you are here, too, Mr. Roland. I do wish you had told me as much."

The door opened and Leyte emerged, which prompted Luno and the knights to bow and leave.

I headed inside with Maylee. Leyte had us sit on the sofa, which I settled right into.

The chamber was furnished with a canopy, a table, and several chairs, but it seemed rather frugal for a queen's personal quarters.

"Roland, this one! This one is softer!" Maylee patted the bed after sitting on it.

"Alias! That is not a place where you should sit."

"Yes, Mother..."

Maylee deflated and made her way behind me as though hiding from the queen.

"Now you're using Mr. Roland as a shield... Really. So it's a rabbit this time?" Leyte exhaled through her nose, obviously exasperated.

"This time?" I questioned.

"Yes, she's brought home cats, dogs, birds, and all manner of other creatures to keep as pets."

"I see. In that case, shouldn't you allow her to keep one, so she'll understand how much work it requires?"

"Were that the case, I would. I'm sure she'll entrust the care to her lady-in-waiting and will only feed it occasionally."

Leyte stretched to try to peer behind me.

"I—I will…I'll look after it. I'll clean the bunny's room and give it water and take it for walks and feed it…and tell it that it's a good bunny."

I doubted that a tsunorabi needed walks.

Although I'd fought them before, even I hadn't taken one in as a pet.

"Alias, aren't you supposed to be an adventurer? You leave the castle in the morning and only come back in the evening. Who will tend to the rabbit during that time?"

"Luno will…"

"And you're already foisting responsibility onto Luno. That rabbit has a horn. Doesn't that make it a monster?"

When Leyte raised an eyebrow, I nodded.

"Yes. However, the little horn is no more threatening than a dog's teeth."

Just as Luno had said, it seemed Leyte had no plans to spoil Maylee.

"I am always telling you, Alias, that you cannot have a pet if you don't take care of it yourself."

"Wahhhh! You're a dummy, Mother! Roland gave me the bunny! I'm keeping it!"

"What daughter calls her mother a dummy? Please leave."

"Uh."

I glanced behind me to find Maylee's eyes filled with tears again.

She had set her mouth into a line, and her little nose was twitching as though she was on the verge of breaking into sobs.

"Lady Leyte, if she hasn't had a pet before, it's impossible to know whether she can care for one. Maylee—Alias is a much more resilient girl than you might realize. She's continued her training the way I taught her, so won't you let her try? She could forgo quests for a while."

Leyte closed her eyes in apparent consideration.

"When I tell you I want a younger brother or sister, you never let me have one, Mother."

"Alias," Leyte chided her, but Maylee continued regardless.

"You always say 'Later, later.'"

That felt like a pretty natural response to something like that.

"Lady Leyte, I believe Alias simply wants a family. Even if it's just a pet."

The queen let out a long sigh and slowly shook her head as though giving in.

"All right. I suppose she may."

"Really?"

"But if I determine that you are not taking care of the rabbit, you won't complain when we release it back into the wild. Do you understand?"

"Yes! Mother, Roland, thank you!"

Maylee rushed out of the room.

"She looked very happy."

"I just hope she really does look after it properly." Leyte smiled wanly and sat by my side. "She may seem like a resilient girl to you, Mr. Roland, but to me, she's my pampered daughter. She's always causing trouble for the people in the castle."

"I think she may become more disciplined with a younger sibling."

"We'll see. But you may be right about her desiring a larger family. That sounds correct, considering how she has been acting."

Leyte called a lady-in-waiting for some tea. Since the queen was still busy, she told me we would just have a cup.

"According to some secret information I have acquired, there are those in support of a different ruler. Some people are opposed to a distribution of power through parliament. I'm sure a few important individuals are hoping to seize authority for themselves, which means the transition isn't going well."

As both a mother and a queen, Leyte certainly had no lack of worries.

Based on what I'd heard from King Randolf, it seemed that power struggles were never straightforward.

"Have you heard of the Welger Company?" I asked.

"Numerous times. Many merchants in our country have memberships with them…"

"There is a possibility they are involved in unsavory activities. Please take care. They may be the ones responsible for any tumultuous situations."

I would likely soon find out from Dey whether the gray wolf poaching was the extent of the Welger Company's misdeeds or if they were connected to darker things.

I needed to know what kind of outfit they were, how large their scope was, and what type of system their organization ran on.

Until I possessed the full picture, I couldn't be rash about my actions.

Chapter 5

That's why I needed someone to collect information for me. While I could have gotten the knowledge myself through torture, Dey was much better at making men sing.

"I wonder if you will be there to help us when we are in trouble, Mr. Roland?"

"I will work to prevent things from reaching that point in the first place, but if it came to that, I'd put a stop to it."

"Ha-ha. I'm happy to hear that, even if I know it's all part of your job."

Leyte wrapped her arms around one of mine, brushed against my knee, and stared into my eyes.

"What I said the other day wasn't meant as a joke. And Alias did say she wants a sibling. Do you dislike forward women?"

"That's not the issue."

I couldn't refuse her the ordinary way.

If things went badly, a woman of her status might cause serious problems if she felt her pride had been wounded.

After a moment, I told Leyte, "I can't reveal details, but I am in a secret relationship with the queen of another country. She has a temper, and I do not know what she might do if she were to find out I had a relationship with you. She may even send out an army..."

The first part was true, though the second half was a fabrication.

Fortunately, Leyte took it at face value.

"Now that would be a problem. So you're already taken by another queen... It seems I had the right idea about you all along," she replied, appearing satisfied with herself. Then she added, "Mr. Roland, you can drop formalities while we are alone together."

"In that case, I'll refrain from them next time."

The conversation was over, so I left her chambers.

6
Starting with Collection Quests A to Z, Part II

◆Bale◆

Formally, the Welger Company was a collection of merchants, but it had a different purpose below the surface. It dealt in illicit drugs and poached monsters, beasts, and plants, selling to whoever would buy.

"Well, that's pretty much all I know."

Bale had revealed what he knew about the Welger Company to Candey. He wasn't certain whether he only knew a part of their activities or if that was everything that went on. The information he'd given was a show of gratitude for Candey saving his life. Yet once Bale came to his senses, he wondered if he should've been so forthcoming.

"Ohh, really. Sounds like you're involved in some very dangerous things."

"This is a secret…just between the two of us," Bale said, flustered, and Candey laughed.

"It's okay. My lips are sealed."

"Well, as far as the company is concerned, I'm dead, so I'm free now."

He was trying to imply he wasn't going to be involved anymore.

"Well, I say I'm free, but I wasn't ever doing anything that big to begin with." Bale's face softened as he derided himself. Candey flicked his nose with her finger.

"Don't say that. I'm sure you're sooo much more important than you even know. You could contribute tons."

"Y-you think so?"

Unable to stand Candey's sincere gaze, Bale cast his eyes down at his hands.

A week had passed since she'd rescued him. Bale occasionally still felt pain, but his wounds had healed well, and he was starting to consider what was to come next.

"Candey."

"What is it?"

"You don't have any family tying you down, right? I actually came from some hick town in the Holy Land of Rubens."

"Oh my, really? I haven't been to Rubens before."

"S-so, why don't you come with me back to my home and—"

Although Bale was the one suggesting it, he felt surprised the words were coming out of his mouth.

Candey had been nursing him this entire time and must have been taking a break from adventuring to do so. Once he recovered, he was sure she would leave.

"I want to thank you properly. Since you saved my life, after all."

"Riiight…"

Candey closed her eyes, evidently considering the offer.

Bale watched her ponder. He could see just how long her eyelashes were. There was something beautiful about them in a way that was different from her smile.

"I'll think about it," she replied.

"What? Really? You're considering it?"

"I'm pretty sure that's what I just said."

She placed a hand on her cheek and smiled, like a veritable goddess.

"Th-thank you. When do you think you'll have an answer?"

"Hmm. I suppose it'll depend on how hard you work."

"W-will it? Then I'll devote myself to it wholly! Once I'm well, I'll—"

"I know you were trying to say you wouldn't get involved in anything dangerous, but I actually like bad boys… I love them merciless and cruel," Candey interjected, looking absorbed in her words. She sighed.

"Th-then you don't care if I commit crimes?"

"I wouldn't mind that at all."

"I'm glad to hear it."

Bale thought she was an odd sort of woman. However, if that was what she preferred, then perhaps it was best for him to return to the Welger Company.

He'd earn far more there than anywhere else, after all.

◆

Chapter 6

Three more days passed.

Candey's nursing had paid off, and though he still felt some pain, Bale could move without impediment, so he returned to his job.

He needed to bring Candey back to his homeland, so his plan was to earn enough for them to live comfortably.

Since the gray wolf incident, Bale had been living with her in her tavern room. He took advantage of her kindness and continued to stay there even after returning to work.

"Welcome home. Are you tired?"

Regardless of whether he returned in the afternoon or late at night, Candey was there to greet him with a heavenly smile. Wonderful though she was, Bale couldn't help but fret about their relationship, so he tried to ask an associate he was comfortable with for advice.

"You go home to an inn and are greeted by a beautiful woman? Seriously? Are you braggin' or somethin'? Piss off."

"I'm not bragging. I'm serious."

"You live with a goddess and get to sleep with her all the time. I'm jealous."

The two men spoke openly, likely because they were out drinking.

"We haven't at all. We're not sleeping with each other."

"What? She too pretty for you or somethin'? You're livin' in a tavern room, right? There's gotta be only one bed."

"There are two," Bale said.

"Huh? Why've you got two of 'em? She's an adventurer, right?

She's basically a nomad, and you're livin' in the room she was already rentin' out, yeah?"

"Uh... So she's an adventurer and hasn't set down roots anywhere...but she's got a two-bed inn room..."

"You're not makin' this up, are you?"

"No! I swear this isn't a delusion!"

"Then the way I see it, this perfect lady of yours has got multiple guys like you under her thumb. While you're out, that slutty goddess or whatever could be foolin' around with other men."

"Don't say that. I don't want to hear it."

"I guess it's possible the place you're stayin' at just happened to have two bedrooms. Could also be that she hates cramped spaces and paid for a larger one that has a second bed."

"The inn does seem packed, so maybe it's that second thing," Bale replied.

"Hey, hold your horses. There's a fourth possibility. If it's this one, then you're in trouble. Look... Don'tcha think it's all kind of convenient? All this stuff you've been tellin' me."

"Convenient? In what way?"

"She saved you from death—that's all good so far. But some women look pretty on the outside and are actually rotten on the inside. Still, she rescued you, so I'm not complainin'." The man tilted his beer stein up, then continued again a moment later. "What got me is after that. Why hasn't she scrammed now that you're workin' again? And why's she waitin' for you to come home? It doesn't add up."

Chapter 6   167

"You idiot...that's obvious. It's because she cares about me," Bale stated.

"Hey...you feelin' all right? You sure she's not tryin' to hoodwink you into somethin'?"

"Of course I am."

"Wait, wait, wait. You haven't been tellin' her anythin' important, have you?"

"What idiot would do that?"

"Right. No way you would've told her about that new work that came in. Ha-ha-ha." The man slapped Bale on the back.

◆Roland◆

It was deep into the night.

While I was resting in the room Leyte had given me, I sensed a familiar presence and left my bed to open the door. I found Dey there, her hand on the doorknob.

"Oh my. I was hoping to sneak in and give you sooo much love while you were fast asleep. Too bad."

"If you're hoping to enter undetected, I'd recommend not using the main entrance."

"But you'd notice right away if I tried that."

"Correct," I said, then I let Dey in. "How did tailing him go?"

Today was our third direct meeting.

We were regularly in contact through the shadows I sent to

retrieve letters Dey wrote. The messages were written in a code known only to Dey and me, so no one else could read them. If anything were to happen to the shadow while the letter was in transit, I'd know immediately. That would also allow me to look into whoever tried to steal the letters.

Fortunately, nothing had gone wrong, and Dey successfully earned Bale's trust.

If I had just wanted to spy on him, I could have had a shadow follow Bale, but there was a chance the Welger Company kept magical barriers around their places of operation, which would keep shadows out. That's why I had to ask Dey for assistance.

Before the hunt on the poachers, I'd explained to Dey that I would let the man in charge get away so I could look into the Welger Company's shady dealings.

"Please find him and earn his trust."

"What a terrible man you are. You know how I feel about you and you're sending me off to entice another man..."

"I never said I was a good person."

"Of course. Sorry if I made you believe I thought as much. I was the one who told you I like how cruel and merciless you are."

I'd allowed Bale, the one responsible for the gray wolf poaching, to go free, and Dey had successfully deceived him.

As expected of a vampire, buttering up a man was a piece of cake for her.

I learned from previous reports that Bale wasn't ranked high in his organization. He'd been in charge of one of many poaching units, and now that his was gone, he'd likely be assigned to another.

Chapter 6

"Things must be going well for him since he returned to the company. I thought he would be going back to poaching, but that doesn't seem to be the case."

"What's his next job?" I questioned.

"Kidnapping, I believe. I can't say that for certain, however. It appears telling him I like bad boys worked. But I had only been talking about you, Master Roland. Oh dear," Dey said. "They're planning to target ex-nobles who might become their political opponents and the children of the wealthy. After the kidnapping, they might manipulate the nobles or ask for a large ransom…"

Nodding, I remarked, "So they're doing it for the money and to keep the new parliament in check. Two birds with one stone, in other words."

"Yes. Evidently, they were poaching to raise enough funds to oppose the government. I'm sure there will be plenty of blackmailed and corrupt parliament members in the future."

"The deeper they ingrain themselves in the economy, the more difficult they will be to eliminate," I commented.

Fortunately, the cancer hadn't advanced far yet.

"They haven't resorted to assassination yet, but that may not be the case for much longer," Dey explained.

"Generally, people are killed so that they can't talk," I replied.

"Also, it seems like no one who goes by those names you told me—Amy, Emilie, Serine, Jance, or Guzel—associates with Bale."

"I see. All right."

My teacher's defining characteristic was that she was a beautiful woman. She was of indeterminate age, and I had no idea what she called herself, but she was powerful. That alone wasn't enough to locate her, though.

Even her beauty could be disguised.

Tallow had spotted her, but I truly hoped she'd left Bardenhawk by now.

"By the way, not all of the money is going toward manipulating parliament. Some of it is being sent somewhere else, although I'm not certain why," Dey stated.

"Really? Please look into that for me, then. I want to stop the cancer from growing while the nation's rebuilding."

Maylee lived here, after all.

"Hee-hee. I suppose the only ones you go out of your way to help are little kids."

I had indeed gotten involved in Lina's affairs as well.

"No, my definition of this is vague, but I'll help people I've spent a lot of time with and those I have a deep connection with… I suppose I care about people in my inner circle."

Dey smiled as she poked my nose.

"Oh, Master Roland, you always come up with novel ways of phrasing things. You can just say they're important to you."

"…I see. I suppose *normal* people would put it like that. Then I will, too."

"I wonder if you would do anything if something happened to me…?"

"You'll be all right. I wouldn't have to intervene because you would be able to take care of it yourself."

"Really? You truly don't understand what goes on in a girl's

Chapter 6 171

heart. You're supposed to say you'll come to my rescue no matter what trouble I'm in."

Dey pretended to be mad as she looked at me with an unimpressed gaze.

"What I mean to say is that I trust you enough that I think you'll be able to take care of things on your own."

I realized that as she stared at me, Dey's eyes had become feverish.

When she hugged me, I held her as well, and the momentum led to us sitting on the bed.

"I'm so happy......," Dey whispered, and she kissed me. "Since we're here today, I need to really show you how much I care for you…"

Dey glanced abruptly out the window and laughed. I also looked over and found a black cat rapping on the glass. She was scowling, her eyes like crescent moons.

"Looks like we have a very terrifying feline in our audience, so I suppose I'll wait for another time."

Dey kissed me again and left. Once I opened the window, Rila made her way inside.

"Really now, I can't let my guard down for the briefest moment…" She snorted angrily.

"You came at just the right time," I told her. "There was something I needed to talk with you about."

"Hmm? Do you feel the need to whisper sweet nothings to me?" she asked, phrasing it as though it were a joke.

"I could do that."

"R-really? I-I would not mind that…"

Rila fidgeted as though embarrassed.

"I'm kidding."

"*Hiss!*" She turned and scratched at me, which I dodged, then I told her what I'd been thinking.

7
The Kidnapping Incident, Part I

◆Rila◆

Roland had informed Rila that Maylee was going to take a break from questing. He also requested that Rila stay by the girl's side for a while.

"Let's go on a walk today," Maylee said.

The room next to the princess's had practically become a tsunorabi pen. Ever since she had decided to bring the animal home, Maylee had been taking care of it there.

She picked up the tawny tsunorabi and gave it a squeeze.

Rila was watching with boredom. "Really now... Why must I be the one stuck watching over the little one...," she groaned, listless, as she scratched at the back of her ear with her foot.

Despite her comment, this was far preferable to sleeping all day.

"Rila, what should we name this one?"

"It's not my pet. You may name it whatever you desire."

"But you're so good at naming things, Rila."

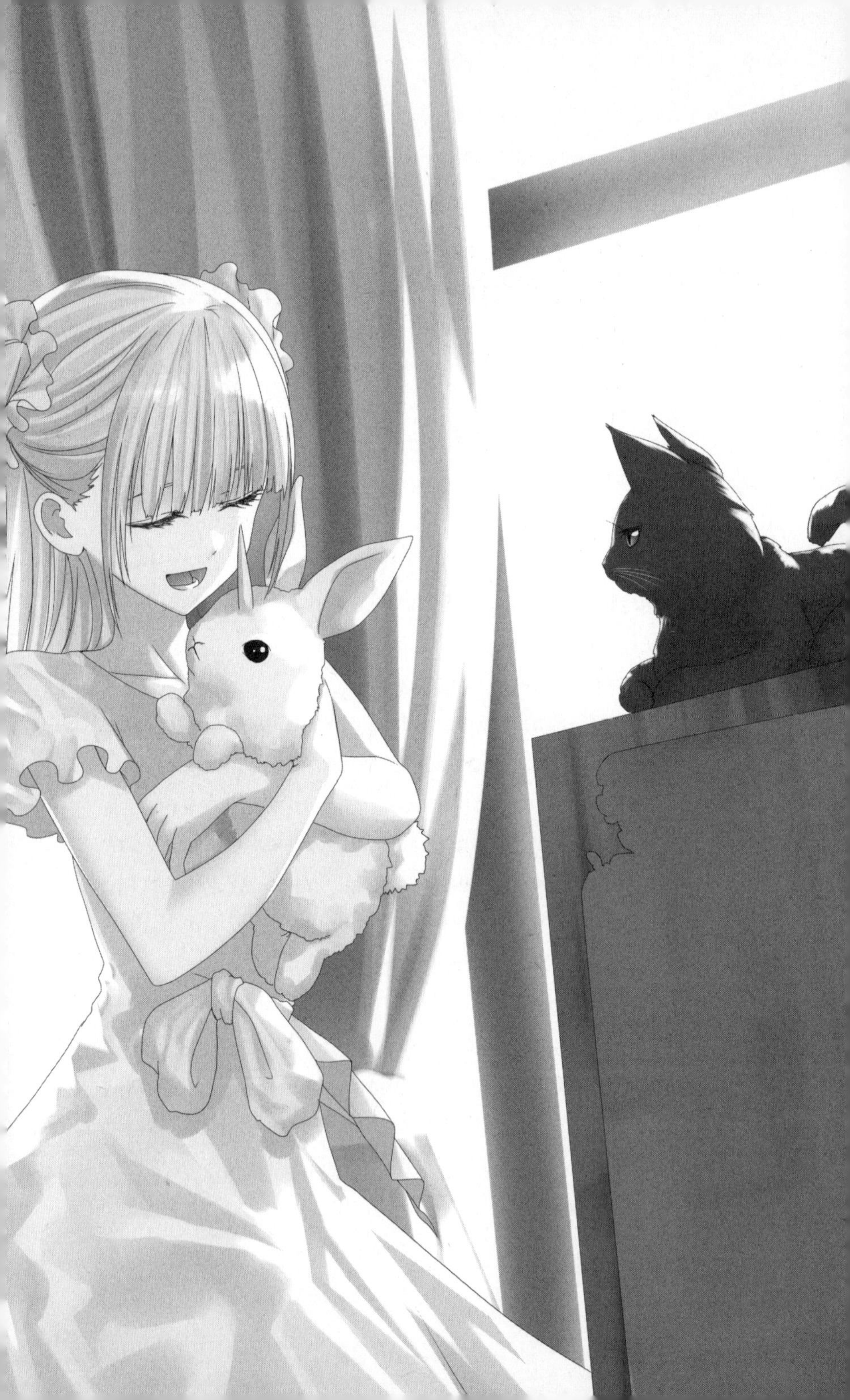

"Then name it Bunnyton. Such a minor monster serves as nothing more than an emergency meal in the woods when one is in trouble."

Rila had enjoyed a very delicious tsunorabi caught and prepared by Roland back when they'd visited his childhood home.

"Well, I suppose they are not lacking...in taste...," Rila muttered as she looked at Maylee.

"Bunnies aren't emergency meals," Maylee chided. "I wouldn't eat them. Bunnyton is basically the same as calling it Bunny, so I'm going to take off the first part and call it Niton. Niton...Niton?"

As Maylee called the tsunorabi, it turned around and looked her in the eye.

Maylee rubbed her cheek into the rabbit's fur.

"Hee-hee, it's so soft and warm and cute... It looked at me when I called, so that must be a good name."

"I suppose you may have forgotten that when I am in this form, I am soft, warm, and quite comforting to hold as well."

"Uh-huh. I know you are." Maylee gave a half-hearted reply and ignored Rila's appeal. Instead, she attached a collar to the tsunorabi and picked up the lead attached to it.

"Let's go on a walk, Niton."

As Maylee strolled off, the rabbit hopped after her.

"Hmm..."

It had a brown and round tail, short legs, a fluffy coat, and a round behind...

"Guh... I-I do not want to admit it, but it is adorable... Even I would like one of my own..."

After accepting defeat, Rila followed after the human and tsunorabi.

To keep from causing a scene, Rila only spoke in her cat form when she was alone with Maylee.

The princess happily visited different sections of the castle and then headed out into the courtyard. She let Niton run free so she could chase after it for fun.

"Oh, Lady Alias, what are you doing?" called Luno, the lady-in-waiting, from a window. She must have been walking down a hall and spotted the princess.

"I'm playing with Niton...the bunny."

"That looks like a great deal of fun." Luno smiled gently. The woman often accompanied Maylee out of the castle, so Rila recognized her well. "Lady Alias, I have just the thing for you to feed your tsunorabi."

"Huh? Really?!"

"Yes, of course. But please do keep this a secret from Lady Leyte."

"Okay! I won't tell Mother..."

"Then please come this way. I will lead you to it."

"Aren't you happy, Niton? You get to eat something yummy."

The tsunorabi wasn't listening to Maylee, nibbling on the short-cut grass instead.

Good food...? For a beast that's happy to chew on any old weed?

Rila was confused, but she recalled her own time as a royal. Many ladies-in-waiting were eager to curry favor with a princess. Luno was probably no different.

The closer one was to the princess, the more likely she would be to listen. There was some amount of self-interest in the kindness.

"I didn't think her that sort of woman, though…"

Rila thought back on how Luno had conducted herself in the past as she quietly approached Maylee to hide under the girl's skirt.

"Eep! Rila, what are you doing…?"

"Quiet."

Rila paid the curious Maylee no mind as she climbed up Maylee's back from within the girl's clothes.

"Your claws hurt," the princess complained.

"Have patience."

"Come, come, Lady Alias," Luno invited again.

Once Maylee was back in the hallway with her tsunorabi, the lady-in-waiting began to lead her along.

"What kind of food is it?"

"If Lady Leyte finds this out, she will scold me. She will say, 'Alias must take care of it herself.' So I will tell you once we are there," Luno replied quietly as she continued forward.

Rila sneakily poked her head out to see where they were.

The shadowy and empty corridor looked a bit darker than usual, perhaps because it was sunny outside.

Quickly, Rila hid back under Maylee's clothes, and no sooner had she done so than she realized the princess had gone limp. Someone caught the girl as her legs gave out from under her.

"…"

There shouldn't have been any other people around. What had Luno done?

"...What shall I do with the rabbit and the cat in her clothes...?"

Rila froze.

Luno had noticed. Her tone had changed, becoming one entirely different from the voice of the lady-in-waiting that Rila knew.

"Well, I would feel bad for the poor princess, so I suppose I will let them tag along."

Luno easily lifted Maylee and began to carry her away.

"If you stay in her clothes, you'll be crushed," Luno cautioned, so Rila emerged. They were on a bed, so she leaped down and looked around her.

It was a humble room that smelled a bit of mildew. Luno had placed Maylee on an old mattress.

The tsunorabi must have still been hungry. Its eyes scanned around, and its nose twitched, searching for food.

Rila could faintly spy the castle from through the window.

Had the woman used magic, Rila would have noticed, even without her mana. However, she hadn't sensed anything, and now they were outside of the palace. Who was this "Luno"? Rila doubted that the real servant could accomplish such a feat.

"Luno," who was cracking her neck, turned to face Rila and the tsunorabi.

"What do cats and rabbits eat again? Well, I guess it doesn't matter. I've done my part."

She swung the key on her pointer finger around and around, then left the room and locked the door.

"So... Maylee's been kidnapped just as he thought she would be. I must report this—"

"Oh! I knew it!" someone interrupted.

"Huh?!"

Rila's shoulders twitched when she heard that. She turned slowly to find Luno staring at her from a window in the door.

"I thought I felt an odd presence. I knew immediately that you weren't any ordinary cat. Are you from the castle? One of the princess's guards?"

"...Something of the sort."

"Hmm. Well, we won't rough her up...or do anything unpleasant to her, so please behave yourself. No one's supposed to die."

"Why did you abduct her?"

"Because we want money. More importantly, how are you doing that? A spell? A skill? Why are you a cat? Did you possess it? Or did you transform into one?"

"It does me no good to tell a kidnapper. You should leave."

"Oh come on, don't give me that."

Rila felt something run through her. She realized that the spell Skill Detection, or something similar, had just been cast on her. If the woman used an Appraisal-type skill, she'd recognize what Rila was immediately...

"...Huh. You haven't become a cat through any skill or magic, then," Luno remarked, sounding disappointed, but Rila sighed with relief.

Thankfully, the skill hadn't been Appraisal.

"So if you don't have a skill and you're a talking cat, that means you're not human."

"..."

Rila glanced at Maylee.

Chapter 7   181

Evidently, this woman hadn't noticed Roland's shadow.

Although the kidnapper was quite perceptive, she had to be ignorant of powerful demonic magic.

"A cat that can talk...no, a monster that looks like a cat? But I don't feel any mana coming from you... So you're a regular cat that's gained the power of speech. How wonderful... Well, I suppose that's enough for now." With that, the woman's eye color and face abruptly changed. "The woman I was pretending to be is still alive. Don't worry. See you later, strange kitty."

After saying that, the impostor Luno walked away.

◆Roland◆

It was a few days before "Maylee" was kidnapped.

"The princess may be in danger," I explained to Rila and Roje. "I've received information from Dey. A merchant guild called the Welger Company is trying to collect a large amount of capital through illegal means like poaching, smuggling, and drug dealing. They're trying to make money as quickly and easily as possible."

Bale had told Dey that his work would be getting busy soon.

"They know targeting noble children in Bardenhawk won't earn them much. They could have targeted nobles in other countries, but it seems they've set their eyes on royalty instead."

Rila nodded. "I see. So you would like us to guard Maylee, then?"

"Let's do all we can, Lord Rileyla!"

"Mm-hmm. Under my leadership, no scoundrels will place even a finger on Maylee."

"That's right, exactly right! I have total faith in you, Lord Rileyla!"

I was surrounded by an overconfident leader and her brown-nosing, foolish follower.

"Rila, I'd like you to watch the princess in your cat form. You'll be smaller, and it should be more convenient."

"Yes, as a feline, I can fit into narrow spaces very easily. It makes it far easier to deceive our foes."

"Stay with Maylee as her pet," I instructed. "We'll say that she's taking a break from adventuring to watch after her tsunorabi. Roje Sandsong, you be her guard."

Both women agreed.

"I will be making a body double for Maylee. Roje Sandsong, I need your help," I said.

"…Are you looking down upon Lord Rileyla and me? These little villains are not even foes to us," Roje replied, but Rila seemed fine with my idea.

"If the worst should happen, this would be our insurance," she said.

"That is exactly right," I added.

"You dare underestimate my abilities as the imperial guard captain?"

Roje harrumphed when things didn't go her way.

"Under normal circumstances, you'd be fine, but I have a concern about all this. If I'm right…things could go bad very quickly."

Roje sniffed. "You're so cautious, human."

"I am," I said. "I want to know who we're up against. If possible, I'd like to get information even Dey wouldn't have access to."

Even as I explained my plan, Roje continued to scowl, likely because Rila was getting involved in this ordeal.

"I want a shadow to act as Maylee's double. You've turned yourself into a dark elf before, so I'm sure you could make a Maylee."

I'd heard this sort of magic existed before, and Roje confirmed it. Unfortunately, this shadow wouldn't be able to send me information directly like other ones.

Pointing at me, Roje declared, "If the kidnapper appears and I repel them, then you will kneel before me! As punishment for making light of my abilities!"

"Fine. If you're able to prevent it from happening, I'll do anything you like."

"You better not forget those words."

Roje was practically radiating confidence.

◆Rila◆

"Hrmm... I really have been caught..."

Roland's goal wasn't to prevent the kidnapping so much as to measure the enemy's strength. In other words, he was gathering information.

If he had actually wanted to prevent the kidnapping, he could have simply guarded Maylee himself.

The real princess was currently safe at the Adventurers Guild.

"The faux Maylee is not lacking in any way compared to the genuine article... I shudder to think he has mastered Shadow to this extent, even though I was the one who taught it to him."

The fake Maylee in the bed seemed as though she were only sleeping.

She was the perfect imitation, which ended up making Rila feel bad.

"I could simply leave her as is, but I do not know what they will do to Bunnyton. I must report to Roland...but will I be able to make it?"

The only possible exit was the window.

If Rila used her claws, there was a chance she could reach it, but it was high up. She called to the tsunorabi that was still sniffing at the ground in search of food.

"You there, Bunnyton, lend me a hand."

The tsunorabi turned around to look at Rila, and then it went right back to its own business.

"Tch. Idiot rabbit...! Then my only option is to figure this out on my own..."

The former demon lord jumped onto the bed and up to the table. As soon as she landed, she leaped for the wall and dug in her claws.

"Okay, I just need to keep at this..."

Her hind legs searched for a foothold but found nothing.

"Guuuh..."

Rila slowly began to slip down the wall. She glared at the tsunorabi.

"Bunnyton, Maylee saved your life! Had she not, you would be jerky. Don't you want to repay her? She is fine now, but if we allow the villains to do as they please, they will hurt her!"

The tsunorabi stared vacantly at the black cat.

"Hmph. Evidently, lesser monsters lack the intelligence to understand speech," Rila spat bitterly. She jumped back onto the bed for a second attempt at her escape. Suddenly, the tsunorabi hopped on the table.

"Oh? It seems I got through to you. Mm-hmm. This is how a pet should be."

Rila joined the horned rabbit on the table and climbed onto its back. The two were about the same size, so she was worried about whether it would be able to make the jump.

"Can you do this with me on your back?"

The tsunorabi didn't answer, and Rila assumed that meant it had no objections.

"You shall hop toward that wall. Then, I shall leap even higher. I apologize for using you as a stepping-stone. But by doing so, I will be able to reach that small window. You needn't worry, for I am presently a cat. I shall demonstrate how spry and agile my legs are in this form. I am counting on your strength."

Rila patted the tsunorabi's fluffy head.

"Three, two, one, and ju—"

The tsunorabi, who hadn't been listening to her in the slightest, bounded off the table.

"Nyaaaaa?! Why are you jumping now?!"

However, the tsunorabi was able to leap quite high.

"Ugh... Nya!"

Kicking off the monster, Rila was able to launch herself higher than her previous attempt.

She clamped down onto the windowsill and scratched at it with her claws, struggling with her hind legs until she could clamber up.

"In the event we succeed without issue, I shall reward you. I, the demon lord, shall bequeath you with two heads of lettuce. You may think of it as an honor. I shall call for help. Until then, please look over the faux Maylee."

With a wave of her tail, Rila slipped through the window's bars and escaped outside.

"I must tell Roland of this! And what is Roje doing?!"

Rila ran as fast as she could back to the guild.

As for Roje...

Rila knew that the elf had been watching the princess until Luno had walked by in the corridor.

"Huh?! What?! Whaaat?! They're gone! Lord Rileyla and the fake Maylee! And even Luno! They're gone?!?!?! How?!?!?!"

She was in a panic after they'd suddenly vanished.

"How could a guard lose the person she's protecting?! Wait, I'm sure they just went to the restroom! ...L-Luno! Where is Luno?! Lord Rileylaaa? Where are youuuu? I taunted that man after he made light of my abilities! Th-this is bad! N-no! Not yet! I haven't fully lost them yet!!"

She had, in fact, lost them.

8
The Kidnapping Incident, Part II

The black cat reached the guild out of breath and was caught by Milia just as she leaped in the door.

"Oh! It's Mr. Roland's cat. Did you come all the way here looking for your owner, wittle kitty?"

Rila ignored Milia and made her way to me.

I had more or less guessed what had happened already.

That idiot elf had confidently told me not to doubt her, and here we were. She hadn't prevented the kidnapping at all.

The real Maylee was watching the guild staff work as part of her social sciences education.

"Can you show me where this place is?" I asked.

Rila nodded.

I got up from my seat and told Iris I would be leaving for a bit.

Once I left the guild, Rila sat on my head and directed me.

"The enemy's home base is in a house right outside the capital. We must hurry or they may change locations."

"I know that."

"Do you know what has become of Roje, knave?"

"She should have been with you, guarding Maylee."

"I cannot find her."

"...She must have lost you."

"We moved from within the castle to that house immediately. It likely happened then."

They had gone from the palace to a house outside of the city?

Even running at full speed, I wouldn't have been able to accomplish that.

"It seems the kidnapper is quite skilled," I remarked.

"Mm-hmm. I did not notice any magic when we were moved..."

"There are skills that prevent others from recognizing when a person casts a spell. That may be the reason."

"Mm-hmm... I see. She also noticed that I am no ordinary animal...and seems convinced I am a monster."

"How likely is it this person is still at the house?"

"It's possible, although she confessed that her job was only to abduct Maylee. Someone else might be keeping watch."

Asking Rila to accompany the fake Maylee had been the correct choice.

Her cat form made it easier to deceive others and enter and exit places at will. On top of that, Rila was levelheaded and made good decisions in the moment.

"That's more than enough information," I said.

If the kidnapper was gone, then this wouldn't be too much of a hassle.

"It's there," Rila stated. I caught sight of an old house dyed orange by the setting sun. "I shall leave dealing with the villains to you and shall return home."

"Okay," I answered.

Rila had escaped through a window, so she didn't know the building's layout. Once I was right by the house, I hid in the shadows of the trees and observed.

"...The faux Maylee aside, Maylee's precious Bunnyton is in there. Would you be kind enough to retrieve it?" Rila asked.

"I thought the tsunorabi was your rival?"

"It's fine. Though it is silent, it understands speech."

Something must have happened after they'd been captured.

Rila nimbly dismounted from my head.

"If you find it necessary, I could investigate the layout," she offered.

"That'd only be necessary if it was anything like the demon lord's castle," I replied.

"Then it seems you do not require me." Rila laughed, then pitter-pattered away.

Everything about the structure suggested it was a normal home. I couldn't see anyone from where I was, but I sensed multiple people inside.

Only one of them was a mage.

The guild master, Tallow, had raised the idea of an underground guild. Perhaps that organization existed in tandem with the Welger Company. Or maybe "the underground guild" was just how the Welger Company referred to itself.

"...Thinking about it won't change anything."

I activated Unobtrusive.

Once I leaped from the shade of the trees, I approached the house at my top speed.

I aimed for pillars and walls that would be out of sight as I swiftly made it to the second floor.

Wreathing my index finger in mana, I tapped on the windowpane four times.

It cracked faintly and, in order to prevent the fragments from creating noise, I caught them on the top of my shoe.

I put my hand through the window and opened it from inside, then snuck in. It was a bedroom.

Inside, a middle-aged man, who seemed to be part of the kidnapping group and was ignorant of my presence, was in the middle of intercourse with a young woman who wore a brand of servitude.

He was so defenseless I couldn't hold back my sigh. This was just so crude for someone who had just abducted a princess, fake or not.

I guess he didn't expect such a quick rescue.

"The unexpected can happen during any plan—that much should be common sense for a villain."

I approached the earnestly thrusting man and rotated his head a hundred and eighty degrees so he could see what was behind him.

"Expect surprises while you're in the middle of things."

I didn't know what to do about the woman, but it seemed her mind was gone. Her breathing was ragged, and she mumbled incoherently. Evidently, she'd only been brought along to fulfill the man's carnal appetite.

I left the woman, grabbed a nearby sword, and unsheathed it.

Picking off my opponents one by one would keep them from knowing I was there, so they wouldn't run away.

Most importantly, however, I was accustomed to killing stealthily.

"Heeey? You done yet? Y'know I'm waiting! You better not be taking multiple turns!"

Someone knocked on the door to hurry things up. I grabbed the doorknob and opened it slowly, then hid in the shadow of the door.

"Oh, it's open... What? At least answer—"

The man took a step in, then another. Then he noticed something was wrong with his naked friend.

"H-hey...? Y-you all right?"

I closed the door. "Sorry for making you wait. It's your turn now."

I invoked my Unobtrusive skill, grabbed the man's jaw from behind, and stabbed through his heart.

"＿＿＿"

He silently screamed and died before I could count to three.

I rolled his skewered corpse onto the bed, checked his belongings, and found a dagger.

This will work much better indoors.

I put my ear to the floor and listened for sounds below.

"Two voices...both men."

The person who had abducted the fake Maylee had to be good—a pro.

Despite her bumbling, Roje had been head of the imperial guard. She was responsible for the unit that protected the demon lord. Anyone who could outwit her was someone to be wary of.

"..."

I couldn't hear what the men were discussing, but they did seem very relaxed for being in the middle of an operation.

Just as Rila had told me, the one who knew what she was doing had likely left already.

I heard a voice growing fainter, then the sound of boots on stairs.

Someone was likely checking in because their companions hadn't come back down.

A man came up, his footsteps echoing down the hall. If I took out this guy, there would be only one left.

I invoked my skill and took him by surprise—attacking the man straight on.

"Why hasn't anyone come back? ...Having some group fun, maybe?"

He hadn't even realized a dagger was sticking straight out of his chest as he cackled to himself.

"Huh…? What? A blade… Blood…?"

I caught the man as his knees gave out, then I gently placed him on the floor to keep from making a sound.

Once I'd confirmed he was dead, I pulled out the dagger. Dark-red blood dripped to the ground in the hall.

"...One remaining."

The last guy undoubtedly hadn't even considered the possibility that his companions were dead on the second floor.

I headed downstairs and found him lounging on a sofa with his feet up. Before entering the building, I'd recognized that one person inside was a mage. This was him.

"Oh? Looks like we have a visitor," he commented lackadaisically upon noticing me.

"Yes. I hope you'll show me some hospitality."

"Based on how you look...I take it you've killed all my associates."

"You mean the other members of the Welger Company?"

"Perhaps that's what I mean."

He was acting very calm for someone with an assassin before him. He didn't even try sitting up. I sensed no traps around him, either.

"I guess I shouldn't have assumed you'd talk easily. I hate using brute force, but if I must..." I approached the man and attacked him with the dagger, which I held in a backhanded grip.

Something stopped the point of the blade, however.

For a fleeting moment, I saw a multicolored wave spread from the tip of the weapon, blocking my strike.

"Do you get it now? You can't touch me."

"...Hmm. Interesting."

"They call my skill Invincible."

He hadn't been watching my movements or even looking at me.

"...So it's an automatic defense, then," I remarked.

"Exactly. I'm surprised you realized after seeing it just once. I'll tell you my name out of respect for those analytical abilities of yours." The man finally stood. He was young and handsome—very different from the others.

"I'm Victor Orlgins. I'm sure you've heard of Iron Wall Victor.

That would be me." He spread his arms dramatically as though he were some stage actor.

"This is the first I've heard of you."

His calm manner wavered for a moment.

"It won't let anything, physical or magical, get to me. My skill is supreme."

If that were true, then he'd won the jackpot.

I knew of several types of defensive skills that triggered involuntarily, and I knew how to deal with them. However, this one surpassed them all.

"Now I understand why you are so relaxed."

"That's right. No matter how anyone attacks me, it'll never work. Even the demon lord couldn't hurt me."

If no one could touch him…

"In that case, you must still be a virgin." When I said that, Victor's face hardened. "…Am I right?"

"No, you just took me by surprise. I wasn't expecting you to say that."

"Don't make excuses. I'm sure you've had to console yourself, since you're always so alone."

"I said you're wrong!"

Based on the conversation, Victor seemed to have a lot of self-confidence… A winner skill like his would make anyone cocky.

"And now the virgin has kidnapped a little girl. You're bringing tears to my eyes."

"It's just a job. My employers recognize talent!"

Victor unsheathed his sword and slashed at me.

I dodged and tried to attack him again, but the multicolored shield was naturally still there and blocked the dagger.

"I've already said it multiple times. No attack will work on me!"

"Yeah. I gathered that."

"What have you gathered?!"

Fwoom, fyoom. Victor waved his sword all over.

"Plenty of things. Now I just need to pray you're not a virgin."

"What a cheap shot. But I'll cut you into pieces soon enough! Guh, I can't get you...!"

"You've got good muscle for blade combat, but that's not enough to touch me."

"Ha-ha-ha, this is entertaining! Let's see if your cheap defense can best my Invincible!"

I cleared my mind, then I slipped near Victor and turned the blade of my dagger on him. It stopped right in front of his nose and eyes.

"Wha?! H-how did you get so close...?!" Victor backed away in alarm.

"Seems I've closed in on you. I knew it. Your Invincible doesn't amount to much."

"You have no idea what you're talking about!"

"That was enough to tell me that you're no virgin."

"Why do you continually ramble about stupid stuff?!"

"You just think it's stupid."

I brushed my emotions aside again and kept my mind empty. Swatting Victor's attacks away, I closed in, this time reaching out for him.

Chapter 8

"*Fguh?!*"

I grabbed his neck and picked him up. He looked distressed and hit my arm, his legs flailing as he did.

"Looks like you're wondering why this happened… Did you truly believe your skill had no openings?"

Victor was turning dark red, and his eyes opened wide for a moment.

"You think no one can touch you? Of course not. Because you're not a virgin. Your skill reacts to others' animosity and ill intentions. Your Invincible would get in the way of sex, otherwise."

"…Tsk!" I wasn't using my full abilities to clamp down on his neck, so he could still speak. "A-all wight. I'll dalk… I'll tell ya eberything I know…"

As someone who'd relied on the protection afforded by his ability all his life, Victory likely wasn't very resilient when cornered.

I threw him onto the sofa. He coughed, taking several big breaths before calming down.

"You're the first person who's ever successfully attacked me… You're amazing…"

I shrugged. "I simply erased any desire to harm you. That was it."

"But you actually did manage to hurt me. I can't believe you can discard your emotions while fighting…"

"I used to work as an assassin."

"An assassin…?"

"Who do you think an assassin kills first?"

"…Your parents or something? Your friends?"

"You've read too much fiction." I forced a smile and continued. "The answer is oneself. You have to kill yourself before anything else. If you can do that, there will be no need to keep your emotions in check. No matter what happens, you'll be as unwavering as a tranquil lake."

"Basically…you haven't got a sense of self…"

"It might be something like that."

"Oh-ho." Victor eyed me with what seemed to be respect.

Since I'd broken through his Invincible, he'd evidently lost all will to fight. There was no chance he'd hit me.

"We'll talk details later. First, let go of your hostage."

"All right."

Victor found the key, then led me down the hall. "This way," he said.

Since we no longer needed the fake Maylee, I uninvoked the shadow.

Victor undid the lock and opened the door.

"Wh-what? She's gone? Where did she—she was right here earlier!"

The room was empty, save the tsunorabi. Its nose twitched.

As Victor panicked, I told him, "Right there. I came to save this guy."

I headed inside and gently picked up the horned rabbit.

After Victor told me everything, I went back to the guild with the tsunorabi.

Rila and Roje were also there, watching the staffers work with Maylee.

When Roje's eyes met mine, she quickly turned away.

"Grrr..." Though she growled at me, she also lowered her head and whispered in a small voice, "...Sorry."

"No, it's fine. I'm glad the insurance was useful."

I clapped Roje on the back and handed the tsunorabi to Maylee, who was looking at me with curiosity.

"Ohh...it's the bunny. You brought him all the way here for me?"

"Yes. I think it wanted to see you."

I tousled Maylee's hair as she squeezed the tsunorabi close.

I thought it would be wise for me to report back what had happened to Leyte, so I headed to her chambers and knocked on her door.

"It's Roland. I have a report for Lady Leyte."

"Please come in."

I opened the door and headed inside to find the queen staring at some documents.

"Are you busy, Lady Leyte?"

"Please, no formal tone. We're alone, aren't we?" Leyte said with a smile.

Switching to my usual voice, I replied, "You're right. Sorry. To cut to the chase, Maylee—Alias was kidnapped."

"What?! But she was just..."

"Yes. I realized what the enemy intended and laid some

preparations ahead of time. To be more accurate, they kidnapped a fake Maylee."

I explained everything that had transpired.

"I can't believe all of that occurred in only an hour. It's lucky you were here to prevent it, Roland. Thank you."

"You don't need to thank me."

"Of course I do. Please let me offer my gratitude. If Alias had been taken, I don't know what I'd have done. I'm sure it would have taken its toll mentally as well…"

"Please don't worry about it. She's…important to me, too."

Dey had told me it would be easier to understand if I used those words.

"Ha-ha. I'm glad someone as amazing as you has taken a liking to my daughter."

According to Victor, it was unlikely there'd be a second abduction attempt now that the first had failed, since the target would be more vigilant than ever. If they were going to kidnap again, it would be more efficient to go after another.

Still, there was no such thing as being too cautious.

"I know she'll object, but I'll have other guards with Roje next time. I'm sure Maylee would prefer people who don't feel like soldiers. If you're okay with it, I know a few adventurers who'd be perfect. I can make the arrangements."

Leyte agreed to my proposal.

While Maylee was in the castle, she would have her bodyguards, and more knights would be stationed outside the palace, too.

I first thought of the pretty girl squad for the guards.

They seemed like they would get along with Maylee. They each had a long way to go, but it was important that the princess's protectors got along and functioned as a unit.

There are several ways to keep a person safe. Being able to fight off the enemy was one, but even if you lost against the enemy, as long as the person under guard was okay, then the mission was a success.

"I heard about something from Victor, one of the kidnappers," I stated.

Thanks to Victor's information and what Dey learned from Bale, I finally had a sense of the big picture.

"There were two groups behind the attempted abduction of Maylee. The first is the Welger Company, and the second are the people with skills that they hire."

Bale had been part of the former. Victor was one from the latter; he'd been hired as an adventurer through the underground guild. Although Victor didn't have details, he believed the person who had kidnapped Maylee had been another contracted adventurer.

The men I'd killed in the house had been from the Welger Company. Victor's job had been to protect them from whoever came to rescue Maylee.

"The one who took the princess was a young woman named Maria. I bet you're wondering why she's not here, right? Originally, she was supposed to stick around, but she changed her contract. She's all about getting her way and only did the kidnapping part because it was interesting. The rest bored her, so she left."

Maria... I hadn't heard that name before.

It had been four years since I'd left my assassin job to join the party of heroes, so she had likely become well-known only recently.

Many who operated in the criminal underworld stopped changing their names once they built up a reputation. Fame brought them more work. Still, it probably wasn't their real moniker, just some fake one.

Just like my teacher, I changed my identity regularly, except when dealing with people I trusted.

I didn't know Maria's common name, so I could only guess what she went by among her close associates.

It wasn't as though top-class operatives openly declared, *I'm called so-and-so. I'm the one who killed that guy.* At least, not the few that I knew.

Plenty of identities disappeared after half a year, so there was no point in remembering them.

I made a habit of forgetting my jobs. Keeping those memories only increased the chance of running into trouble. People who try to hide their recollections and those who can't remember at all acted differently. The best camouflage was to erase the experiences from your mind.

Still, I could recall some jobs if I saw the faces of my previous clients.

"I looked into the Welger Company a bit more," Leyte told me. "Forty percent of their money has come from unreputable sources. Unfortunately, with so many merchants in their ranks, they're functionally untouchable."

"There's also the question of just how much of the organization is corrupt. I don't think you need to assume dismantling is the only solution."

Leyte nodded. "Of course."

"Victor accepted the job through a group that was acting for the Welger Company. This is no amateur operation. He said more dangerous people are bound to appear."

"More..." The queen's face clouded over with evident worry.

"We'll constantly track their movements and work to make sure this doesn't become a serious matter," I assured her.

"Thank you. You truly are reliable, Roland."

With that, I concluded my report.

On the way back to the guild, I thought of Victor. I'd wondered how much he'd be willing to confess, and it turned out he gave me everything he knew.

"*Are you sure you should be doing this?*" I'd asked. "*Should you tell me all of this?*"

"*I don't mind. Since you're probably the only guy who could kill me.*"

"*Invincible, huh... Seems like a very useful skill.*"

"*Right? So...you're part of the Adventurers Guild, right? I'd like to work there sometime. Sounds like more fun than this stuff.*"

"*You wouldn't be paid as well as working underground.*"

"*I don't mind that, either.*"

Victor hadn't been part of the plan to kidnap Maylee, and someone had executed the scheme.

He'd only been present to prevent a rescue, and since the princess wasn't in the house, he saw no reason to fight.

"If you're interested, then come to the capital's Adventurers Guild. Your abilities would be welcome there," I said. Then I left.

Unlike me, Victor likely was a good person on the inside. A part of me was expecting him to wander into the guild eventually.

◆

He never showed up.

A week went by, and we found his corpse. A fisher discovered the body near a lake.

Close inspection revealed he'd been stabbed a single time with something like a dagger—possibly an even smaller weapon.

I was impressed by the technique. Victor probably hadn't suffered, which was the one silver lining.

That man had put too much confidence in his skill. Although, I imagined it was hard not to, considering how powerful Invincible was. For all that might, it still had a weakness, however.

There was no such thing as being invincible.

Victor had reaped what he'd sown. It made me realize again that the underground world was also not to be underestimated.

After the kidnapping incident had been settled, the pretty girl squad stopped by the guild with perfect timing, and I raised the idea of the guard work.

All of them, including the leader, Eelu, had immediately told me they were happy to do it.

The castle grew livelier when they started watching over Maylee.

"Master Roland, please listen. May tried to grab my tail to pull it."

Lyan came to my room after breakfast, half in tears.

I patted her on the head to console her, and Maylee dashed in almost immediately after.

"Roland, I didn't! I didn't pull it. I really didn't! It was just so fluffy that I wanted to touch it."

"It doesn't matter what happened. Please just get along."

Since all four members of the pretty girl squad had to stay with Maylee, the remaining three quickly arrived.

"May…is tired of Niton… She wants Lyan now," Sanz explained quietly.

It seemed Niton had become the tsunorabi's actual name.

"I haven't gotten tired of Niton. I'm looking after him properly," Maylee argued.

"You forgot to feed him earlier, and I had to do it," Eelu countered with a smile, and Maylee realized in surprise that she actually might have forgotten.

"P-please don't tell Mother… She'll take Niton away."

"It'll be fine. We won't say anything to Lady Leyte," Eelu assured her. As Maylee exhaled deeply with evident relief, Eelu continued, "But make sure you focus on more than just adventuring. You need to study, too."

"Ugh…"

"If you can't… I don't have to finish that sentence, now, do I?"

When she caught sight of Eelu's intense grin, Maylee turned to me. "Roland, Eelu is being mean…"

"She's not. You're just trying to shirk your responsibilities."

Lyan poked her head out from behind me. "That's right. Because you always try to skip out on things right away."

"…But you're always behind me playing with Niton and making a big deal out of it. It's so annoying."

"Lyan, you need to stop bothering Maylee."

"Sanz, do you always have to be so forthcoming? Don't tattle to Master Roland."

In a twist, Sanz had betrayed Lyan.

Actually, Lyan had been the one to snitch on Maylee first.

"Now, Princess Alias, it's time for your homework." I shooed all five of them out, which made Maylee frown.

"But you always go straight to work, Roland. And then you won't play with me at all when you get home."

"Ha-ha-ha, you've made a lady sulk, Master Roland," Eelu remarked, seemingly amused. Roje and Su had been watching everything from outside the room.

"Right now, your job is to study," I said.

"N-no! I'll study if you play with me."

"I'll play with you if you study."

"Grrrrr… Fine. Pick me up and take me to my room."

It didn't seem like Maylee would permit any further compromises, so I did as she asked, carrying her in one arm.

"That's so unfair. I want Master Roland to carry me, as well," Lyan complained.

Chapter 8   207

"…I call his back."

Sanz climbed onto me.

"Then I'll take an arm, too."

Eelu linked arms with me, and Roje pointed at me.

"Lord Rileyla, do you see his lack of decorum? He surrounds himself with women and ogles them… That is this human's true nature." As usual, Roje was trying as hard as she could to ruin my reputation.

Rila, who was below our feet, yawned and didn't seem to care.

"I think that Master Roland is always proper."

"Su, why you little… You're an elf, and yet you side with the human…!"

"Race shouldn't matter. You have such antiquated views, Lady Roje."

Outside the room, Roje and Su were staring daggers at each other.

As fellow elves, I'd assumed they'd get along, but I'd been mistaken.

Everyone started speaking all at once, and since it didn't seem like they would be settling down anytime soon, I left with just Maylee, pretending I hadn't heard any of them. We reached her room.

"Make sure you work hard at studying."

"Okay."

Rila slipped in as well.

"Her guards are not here, but she should be fine for now. Bunnyton and I will be able to handle things." She seemed awfully confident. I very much doubted they'd be able to handle anything. "Despite how he may seem, Bunnyton is a dedicated soul who believes in the ways of the pet."

"What in the world happened between you and that tsunorabi?"

"There is more beauty in leaving such things unstated. Entrust Maylee to us. You may go."

"See you later, Roland," Maylee said.

"Right, I'll be going."

Rila and Maylee saw me off as I went down the hall. When I reached the princess's guards, who were still arguing, I told them to get back to work.

Milia and Iris were waiting for me in front of the castle gate.

"You're late, Mr. Roland. What were you doing?"

"Babysitting," I replied.

Iris grinned. "Ha-ha-ha. Sounds like you had your hands full."

"No, it wasn't too bad."

The three of us made our way down the gently sloping hill toward the city.

This country had a long way to go before things were stable again, but if the Adventurers Guild grew, public order would settle in and fewer people would suffer.

When I thought of it like that, I couldn't help but feel motivated to do my job.

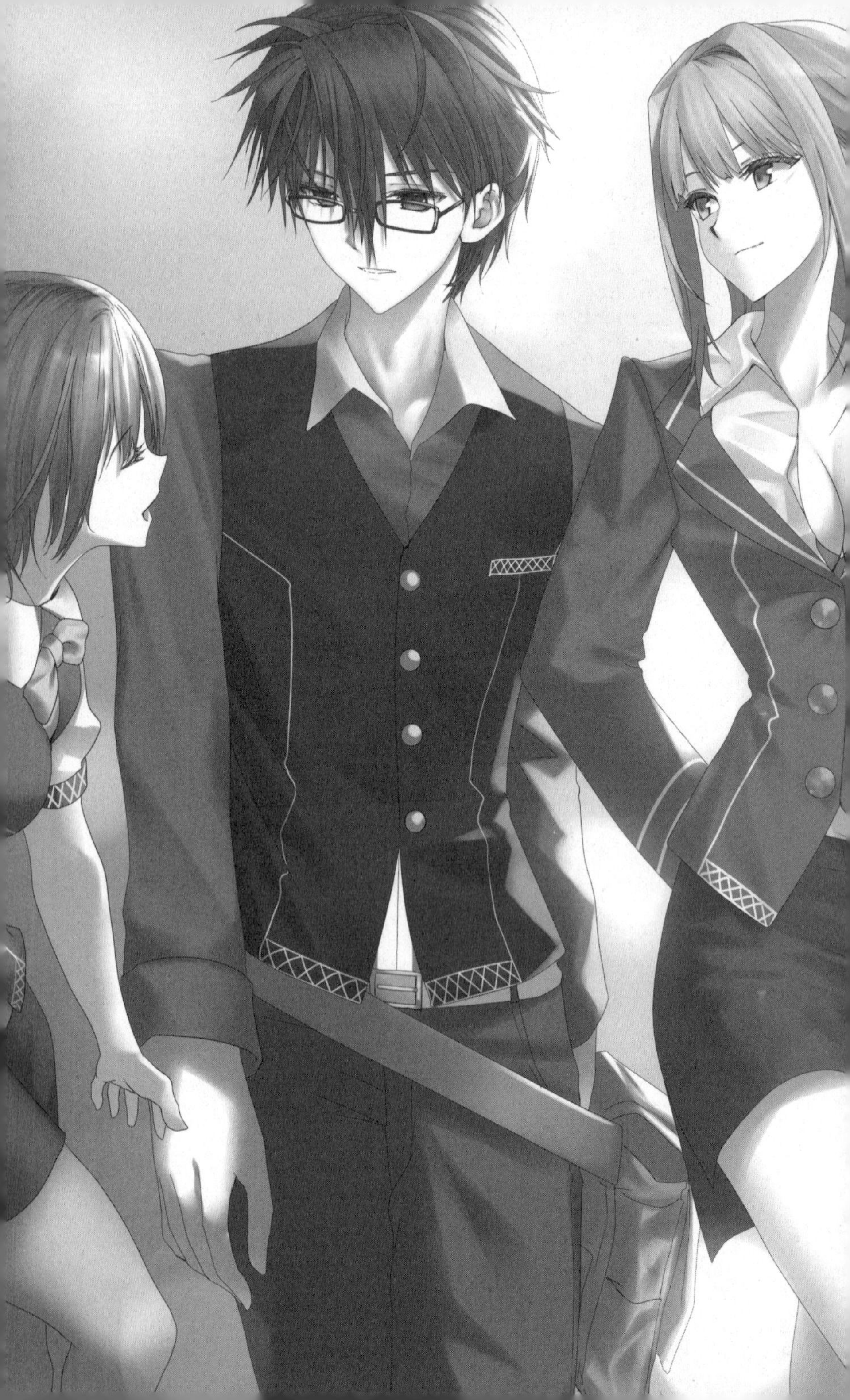

9
By the Manual

Nothing of note had occurred since we'd prevented Maylee's kidnapping. The days passed uneventfully.

"There haven't been any significant movements lately. Looks like your flawless plan to prevent the kidnapping has been a huge success," Dey had informed me with a snicker. She'd been looking into the Welger Company's actions. "But it seems like you did things so perfectly that they're on high alert. Things might not go as well as last time," she added.

I'd never slack when it came to preventing a kidnapping, so our enemies would've ended up cautious no matter what I'd done.

There was a possibility they'd suspect a traitor among them and try to root out who it was. If that happened, it would be best for me to extract Dey before things went south.

"I'd like to take higher-ranking quests."

"As I said…gathering jobs are very important, so—"

While talking with a female adventurer while on reception duty, I overheard a conversation from the neighboring booth.

"I know that I'm good at gathering, but surely you have other quests that are, well, y'know? Like something that would require collecting items in a dangerous area."

"I've already explained that's not possible… Your combat abilities suck too much for that."

The staffer muttered that last part, but the male adventurer must have heard it.

"Hey, what did you just say?!" he demanded.

"Oh, uhh."

One of the new Bardenhawk guild employees was dealing with the male adventurer.

After asking the female adventurer I was assisting to wait, I tried to get the attention of the staffer next to me.

"Oh, sir…"

The junior employee was looking at me as though I was his personal savior. The adventurer, however, glared with murderous fury.

"My colleague was incredibly rude to you. I am very sorry," I said, bowing my head. The junior employee followed suit and stuttered out an apology.

"If you wouldn't mind, I can help you find something," I suggested.

"All right. Sheesh. Nobody's willing to give me good quests even when I go up in rank just because of my combat abilities."

The disgruntled patron was a local adventurer who looked to be in his twenties. I thought he was rather old to be pouting in public.

"May I see your adventurer permit?" I asked.

Lendar Hawkins. D rank. Quest log…mostly E and F rank. Ratio-wise, seventy percent were F rank.

His skill was called Division.

"..." I glanced at the adventurer in front of me. Then I looked at the more detailed documents about Lendar in my hands.

Hmm.

Division allowed you to make a few of copies of yourself. The only issue was that the combat abilities of the doppelgängers lowered with every subsequent duplicate.

"I'm in D rank. Why won't you give me any quests in my rank?"

I looked at the stub on the counter, which was for an E-rank gathering job.

Lendar was less likely to encounter monsters on such quests, which meant the junior employee was doing things by the book. If anything, all the worker had done wrong was speak his true feelings.

"I'm sure adventurers believe meeting the printed criteria is all that matters, but that isn't the case for guild staffers. We need to take into account your abilities, your success and failure rates, and whether you'll come back to make a report, regardless of the results. All of that goes into how we distribute quests. Even if you meet the basic requirements, it doesn't mean a thing if, in actuality, you can't handle the task."

"Ugh... But if I don't get a chance to at least try..."

It was difficult to give a D-rank quest to an adventurer without much fighting ability when it was likely they would encounter an enemy. In other words, Lendar's Division skill meant he had the perfect assistants for gathering jobs that demanded high numbers.

"While I can't condone my coworker's attitude, he was giving you the right sort of quest. It's common for adventurers to overestimate their abilities and take on something they never come back from. Would you want that for yourself?"

"Uhh," Lendar groaned. Then he went silent. Everything up to this point had been done according to protocol, but this was going to be resolved *my* way.

"You have a point when you say that it's impossible to know until you try."

The junior employee and Lendar both stared at me with clear surprise. I suppose they had thought the matter was settled.

Until he went on a D-rank quest, Lendar wouldn't know how dangerous one could be. That meant he'd always be dissatisfied, but we still couldn't give him one.

"Allow me to arrange a D-rank quest for you," I told him.

"A-are you sure, sir?" the junior guild worker asked me.

Lendar blinked a few times. "Really…?"

I nodded.

"Yes, recklessly taking on a job is different from going into a challenge informed. But I have one condition. You have to do it with her."

Juiz, the female adventurer I'd been assisting earlier, looked startled when I mentioned her. Her eyes went wide, and she pointed at herself.

"Huh? Y-you mean me? But I'm in E rank…"

Under normal circumstances, I'd have to refuse Lendar. However, when people teamed up, it was possible for them to bolster each other. Synergy, you might call it. A party's combined talents were more than the sum of their parts.

That was exactly what I had in mind for these two.

"Ms. Juiz has a skill that allows her to strengthen those around her."

"Y-yes... It doesn't have much range, though, and it's a very narrow area. It's a terrible skill and has a long cooldown, so I can't use it continuously... Plus, its activation time is half the cooldown..."

Her confidence waned as she explained the ability.

I was hardly one to talk, but it *was* a weak skill. According to the documents in my hand, its range was a diameter of one meter, and it couldn't be triggered again for an hour after activation. Juiz's magical aptitude was also low, so she mainly took E-rank quests.

"If you would be willing, Ms. Juiz, how about teaming up with Mr. Lendar to attempt a D-rank quest? I think that it will be a great experience for you both."

The guild's notes on Lendar said he'd never worked with another adventurer before, likely because of his skill. On the other hand, Juiz jumped from one party to the next pretty frequently. Her strengthening skill made her an attractive get, but it probably wasn't too useful in practice.

"Then...I look forward to working with you." Juiz turned to Lendar and bobbed her head.

"Same here."

After exchanging awkward greetings, the two shook hands.

The junior employee straightened up to his full height and seemed enthusiastic as he observed how I handled things.

"Please come this way," I said.

I guided Lendar to a seat in front of me and gave a quick explanation.

"I will grant you both the same quest. Ms. Juiz, since you're an E ranker, I normally wouldn't be able to assign this quest to you, but you will be compensated should you succeed, so please don't worry."

With that, I gave them a *yamabanasou*-gathering job, which was D rank.

Yamabanasou was a poisonous plant used as a paralytic agent in hunting. It was as dangerous as it sounded.

"With your powers combined, I think it shouldn't be an issue," I stated, and then I saw the two adventurers off.

"...Sir, do you really think they'll be okay?" the junior employee inquired, evidently worried. "Doesn't *yamabanasou* only grow deep in the forest? They're not alone, but that doesn't make it any less perilous."

"Mr. Lendar has fulfilled many gathering quests, so he has ample knowledge and experience dealing with the woods. You shouldn't discount his intuition."

I'd developed a keen sense for when things might go wrong while working as an assassin, even when there was no basis for judging.

"But their abilities to deal with any enemies..."

"You're right. Alone, they would undoubtedly be in danger. However, if Lendar uses Division and Juiz uses Strengthen, Mr. Lendar's duplicates will become powerful fighters."

The more doppelgängers he produced, the weaker each successive one was—at a rate of around 30 percent, apparently. Still, monsters that appeared on D-rank quests were easy enough to surround and best to take out with brute force alone.

"I see. So adventurers can handle more difficult jobs by working together!" the junior staffer exclaimed.

"It depends on the time and place, though. In this instance, Lendar is with a woman who can empower his base strengths, so he'll be able to fight confidently."

"Does this mean I shouldn't do things by the book, then?"

"No, the manual is perfectly fine. If you follow it, you shouldn't run into many problems. Just know that there are exceptions to everything."

"I see…strength in numbers…and special cases…"

My junior colleague was writing down what I'd said. I suddenly felt embarrassed.

Lendar and Juiz returned in the evening.

"Thank you for your work. That was quick. How did it go?" I asked. The two smiled in reply. Lendar, the adventurer who hadn't been satisfied with the quests that had been arranged for him, and Juiz, who'd possessed little confidence in her abilities, now seemed very different people. Their troubles had melted away.

I appraised the *yamabanasou* they'd gathered—my first inspection since acquiring the Plant Master license.

"Yes, this is all certainly *yamabanasou*. And it's in good condition as well."

"Mr. Lendar told me it's better to dig the plants out of the ground than to pick them from the stems, so it's thanks to him."

Lendar looked flustered at the remark.

"We did have to battle, but thanks to Juiz, I could handle opponents I'd normally run from."

"It seems you didn't have any difficult fights, then," I said. "I'm glad."

"That's right," Juiz replied. Then she asked, "So you can even do appraisals, Mr. Argan?"

"Yes. I'm qualified to inspect plants."

"You really can do everything."

"Not everything, just what I'm capable of."

"H-he's so cool...," Lendar praised, and I heard the junior employee behind me say the same. "Juiz and I talked about having you arrange another quest for us on the way home, Mr. Argan."

"Can we count on you again?" Juiz inquired.

"Certainly."

After that, I paid the two their due and saw them off. Evidently, I would be seeing them together again soon.

As soon as I was free, the junior employee rushed over and bowed to me.

"Um, sir, I would like to become your apprentice! Please take me on!"

"...You don't have to go that far. I'll teach you what I can regardless. That's a senior employee's duty, after all."

"Y-yes, please do!!"

Depending on the location, circumstances, and party members, even a weak skill could shine.

10
Princess Alias's Adventure Journal

"Princess, please be careful."

The servants who had gathered in front of the castle gate courteously bowed as they saw Maylee off.

"See you later!" she said enthusiastically, and her protectors and servants each bid her farewell in reply.

"Hmm? Leyte is waving from the window, Maylee," Rila said. She was currently in her black cat form and standing by Maylee's feet. The princess looked up and saw her mother by a window in the queen's chambers. She waved back, then set out into town.

"I wonder what kind of quest they'll have me do today."

"Well, you are a mere fledgling. Doubtless, he will not allow you to take a true adventure," Rila replied, quite meanly, then she chuckled.

"He has informed me you will look for a lost item," Roje stated while flipping through a notebook. She must have taken notes.

Maylee's cheeks puffed up.

"But I wanna use a lot of Back Slashes."

"It's simply what we call working your way up. Have patience."

"...That is hardly convincing coming from you, Lord Rileyla," Roje quipped.

"Did you say something?"

"Not at all! Nothing!" Roje jumped to attention, which made Maylee giggle.

◆

"I have a lost-and-found quest for you today. The object is very precious to the client, but you can take your time with this. Regardless of the outcome, please report back on your progress in the evening."

Just as Roje had said, Roland had, in fact, set up a simple retrieval job for Maylee.

"I wanna do something else," she whined in vain, as Roland didn't listen.

He quashed all her complaints with remarks like "Don't get ahead of yourself, F ranker." Maylee felt close to exploding from all the pent-up disappointment.

"There's no such thing as a good or bad quest. That's what it means to work as an adventurer," Roland commented.

From below, Rila added, "Please do not grumble so. If you keep at it, you will eventually reach E rank. Then you will be able to take the jobs you prefer."

"Hmph... I'll do it, but this is the last one!" Maylee said, which earned her a gracious smile from Roland.

"Princess Alias, you still need five more quests before you can rise in rank," he reminded her.

"Ugh!"

Maylee stomping around as she accepted her work had become

a guild staple. Other adventurers watched the familiar sight with amused grins.

"Come now, Lady Alias, let us go." Eelu, one of the princess's guards, tugged at her hand.

"Master Roland is busy with work. You can't bother him," Lyan cautioned.

Left with no other alternative, Maylee left the guild, taking a moment to turn back and stick out her tongue at Roland before she was gone.

"Maylee, you must refrain from undignified displays," Rila admonished her, but the girl only turned her face away in a snub.

"It's Roland's fault."

Rila could only smile forcibly in resignation.

"Lady Alias, here is the information we have." Su showed Maylee the notes she had collected when they had accepted the quest. The client was a woman in her thirties. She'd lost her hair ornament, a keepsake from her mother, on First Street, the primary thoroughfare in the capital.

"…"

Maylee's fingers traced over the family broach she carried. The gift from her mother had never left her side.

"You must put a bit of effort into this one." Rila stoked the fire rising within Maylee, who nodded solemnly.

"Rila, can you find it by sniffing for it?"

"I am no dog. You must use your own wits."

"Hmph… Then, Rojey, do you have detection magic that can search for it?"

"I cannot use any such spells."

"Aww..." Maylee looked put out and at a loss. Even the pretty girl squad offered nothing. This was proving to be a true roadblock.

She stared at the quest documents for a while, then abruptly realized something. There was a page that described the accessory's features and even had a drawing of it.

"Rojey, can I borrow your notebook and something to write with?"

Roje gave her a pen and tore out several sheets from the notebook in response. Using a wooden box on the side of the road for a table, Maylee copied the drawing and wrote a short description of it.

"One..."

Then she drew another on a second sheet and a third. Though the sketches were crude, she'd replicated the ornament's features as described.

Her guards asked no questions and instead only watched Maylee as she worked.

"Done!"

Maylee had created five flyers. In truth, she wanted more, but this would have to do for now. With no time to lose, she hurried to a restaurant.

"Ah, Your Highness. What business do you have here today?"

"This is important, so I'm looking for it."

Maylee gave the shop owner one of the flyers.

"I understand. So you want me to ask if any customers have seen it?"

"Yes, thank you."

Then she left and distributed the remaining posters to the most well-connected merchants in town.

"Oh-ho. I see," Rila remarked, as though she were impressed.

"Well, Roland did say I could take my time," Maylee answered.

"Getting others to aid you... How shrewd."

Maylee felt overjoyed when Rila treated her like an adult.

"This will solve things faster than me doing it alone."

"You're so smart, Maylee...," Lyan let slip.

Maylee did the same for two more days. When she went to the eatery to ask if they had any information, the shopkeeper had something wrapped in a handkerchief.

"Your Highness, is this perhaps what you were looking for?"

When he opened the cloth, a hair ornament exactly like the one described in the notes was resting in his hands.

"Oh, that's it! Where did you find it?"

"Someone picked it up. I think he was planning to keep it, but as soon as he learned the princess was searching for it, he brought it here in a hurry."

"Thank you."

"You're quite welcome. I'm glad it was found."

They left the eatery and told the other shopkeepers what had happened before heading back to the guild.

"Roland! I found it!"

"Hmm. Good job."

Maylee reveled in her triumph, flaring her nostrils and puffing up her chest.

Later, they would inform the owner that the missing article may have been found so she could confirm it was hers. However, since it looked exactly as depicted in the owner's drawing, Roland said he was sure it was the right one.

"Looks like you've got a good head on your shoulders," Roland commented.

"Huh?"

"Rila told me everything. I asked them all not to intervene with your quest. A princess always has people by her side. If you don't think for yourself, you will soon find yourself depending on others."

"So that's why they did that?"

Maylee turned to her five guards waiting behind her. They all laughed nervously.

"Even though it doesn't involve fighting, finding a lost object is rather difficult. Usually it's been stolen, or the owner's memories are too vague to give enough clues."

When Maylee realized Roland was complimenting her, she began to feel more pride in herself.

"Asking for help from the shopkeepers who are good at information gathering to spread the word is worthy of commendation. You did well."

Roland gave her a pat on the head, which made her legs feel like jelly. Maylee couldn't bring herself to look straight into his black eyes when he was staring at her so intently.

"What good will come of making a child fall in love with you?" Rila said with some exasperation after hopping onto the countertop.

"All I did was praise her."

"Ha-ha. A man up to no good. That is what you are."

"In what way?"

Maylee felt a slight pang in her chest when she saw the two speaking so casually and intimately. She recognized she wasn't Roland's favorite.

"...I'm going home now!"

When the princess stood and tried to run out of the guild, Roland called, "I hope you'll put just as much effort into your next F-rank quest."

And suddenly, she was right back to feeling happy again that he was relying on her.

"No!"

However, Maylee stuck out her tongue. She ignored all objections and hurried off with her guards dashing after. Despite what she had said, Maylee was smiling.

◆??◆

"...Amy, it seems Princess Alias's kidnapping was a failure," Count Barbatos Guerrera muttered in his office, as though to himself.

A woman appeared from behind him.

"I'm aware. I was the one to settle the matter, after all."

"Yes, of course. I'm sorry for repeating myself. Bad habits die hard."

The count signed documents even as he conversed, and the woman sat down on the edge of his desk.

"According to Victor, the man who arrived to save her was quick, almost as though he knew she'd been taken. Also, Princess Alias wasn't in the room she was supposed to be trapped in."

"She wasn't? Tut, tut, Amy. What did you capture then? Hot air?"

"I'm certain it was the princess… But the real issue is that someone knew about the abduction in advance. He must have come up with a counterplan of—"

"Excuses don't make for a good look."

"This only became such a chore because the company was involved. The more people in the know, the easier it is for information to leak. I hardly think I'm responsible for the failure."

"Well, you have a point. They have many heads, but not many brains."

"The man who came to rescue her saw through Victor's skill almost immediately. After fighting a man he didn't know for only a minute, he understood everything he needed to win. We're up against someone with skill. They're dangerous. Enough so that even I need to be on my guard."

Count Guerrera's pen abruptly stopped.

"…How unusual. You rarely praise others." He hardly cast a glance at the woman sitting on his desk as he silently read over his documents. "I sent you a message as a last resort because I couldn't get in contact. You never read it, did you? I'm so sad at the thought, Amy. I went to such great pains drafting you that love letter."

"Oh, well that's too bad. But consider yourself a lucky man, Barbatos. Had it been a love letter and had I read it, I would have publicized the thing."

The count wasn't listening. Instead, he whispered to himself as he read his papers. Then he set them down and returned to writing and signing.

"You could simply use the assassins I selected for you as guards. Even if that special public welfare division comes, you should be safe. The assassins will protect you."

"I would much rather you guard me, though. I'm the type to work his ace to the bone. There's no point in a trump card that's never played, right?"

"Will you be able to gather the funds?"

"Not immediately, but I think we have good prospects. It would have been much easier had the kidnapping been a success."

"Oh, don't be so disagreeable. You should be happy that the outlooks are good. I was surprised to hear what you've been up to after not seeing you for such a long time. You've become quite ambitious in my absence. Ha-ha."

"Does quashing the Felind Kingdom really sound that ambitious?"

"I was surprised by the meticulousness of your scheme and its scale. You plan to trap the Bardenhawk parliament under your thumb, so you have their backing. It seems you've put a lot of thought into this, even though you yourself are a Felind aristocrat."

"Now is the best time to curry favor with nobles, since they're all worried about King Randolph punishing them. Did you know,

Amy? More aristocrats have dirtied their hands than kept their noses clean. Naturally, they would be terrified of being part of the next purge. With a man like that as king..."

"Then what?"

Count Guerrera paused in his work and met Amy's eyes. "Then I will need to make him disappear."

"That's no simple task. The hero lives in Felind castle—that great, honest-to-god hero who saved the world."

"Exactly right. That hero-princess will eventually become an obstacle on our path to crushing Felind. That's why I wanted to meet with you directly to talk this over, Amy."

"..."

"I prefer to use my aces whenever I can. Keeping one up my sleeve would be a waste. Still, this job may be too big, even for you."

"Spit it out. If it seems interesting, I'll do it."

"It's nothing so petty as kidnapping. This time, I'd like you to assassinate our hero."

"How very interesting."

Count Guerrera sighed, disappointed.

"That's a bad habit of yours—basing your work on whether it's entertaining. When did you become such an odd assassin?"

"Who can say?"

Count Guerrera shook his head, but clapped his hands together, as though he'd suddenly remembered an important point.

"I had something else to ask you about. Remember when you told me that you knew the person behind the whole disaster at the underground arena?"

"Yeah. And?"

"Well, I was glad to hear that was the case after seeing the butcher's arm fly off. I could hardly believe something so quick was the work of a single person. Yet you claimed to see him while you were watching next to me. Quite a few wealthy folks were looking forward to that event, you know."

"What do you want this time?"

"Don't rush me. I like savoring the moment when I have conversations with beautiful women."

Amy brushed him off, saying, "Sure, sure."

"After that, the arena was destroyed in a blast due to some force. And Lord Moisandle... No, I suppose he no longer has a title. That was stripped along with his territory. Anyway, some man broke into his home and ruined everything. Don't you think it's strange, Amy? It must have something to do with all this special public welfare division nonsense."

"So this culprit that's got all the nobles fretting is part of the special public welfare division?"

"Yes. And if they're your acquaintance, I'd prefer that you told me."

"Not happening. I don't know where he is. Even I can't find him."

"I sent you that letter hoping you would resolve this, but if you refuse, then I must resort to other measures."

The count placed a blank sheet on his desk and wet his pen with ink.

"He is guilty of disrupting the underground arena. I want you to describe what he looks like and give me anything else you know about him."

"What do you intend to do?" Amy questioned.

"I'll submit a request to the underground guild. I'm sure a bounty will turn up something on him."

Count Guerrera was trying to pressure Amy, but she seemed unbothered.

"I doubt it'll work," she said, but proceeded to tell him all she could think of.

> Reward: Forty million
> Age: Twenties
> Sex: Male
> Eyes: Black
> Participated in dismantling underground arena
> Other information: Possesses skill that obstructs his recognition

"Ah, right, and the most vital bit: What's his name?"

"He often goes by Hamel, Bjorn, Leon, or Kruger. And also… Roland."

"Having his name might not be of much help, then. They all sound very common," the count remarked, but he added them nonetheless.

Afterword

Hello. I'm Kennoji.

Thanks to you, the series is still going, and we've already made it to publishing the fourth volume.

In this book, the protagonist, Roland, gets a request to set up an Adventurers Guild in another country. I'm sure those of you who read the story know this, but Roland realizes there's a plot lurking in the shadows. And that will be covered more in the fifth installment of the series. I personally like the overall flow of the fourth and fifth volumes. "Yes, yes, this is exactly the kind of stuff I like." That's how I felt as I was writing this. If I say more, I'll spoil it, so I won't. However, I'd like to give myself a pat on the back for the interesting way it all develops.

If that interests you, I would be so happy if you'd eagerly look forward to the next book.

I think that my own anticipation is peeking through in this afterword (probably), so allow me to change the subject.

I'm sure some have noticed the commercials on TV for this book. That might have been the happiest event of the year for me.

The manga adaptation has also had a wonderful reception and will be receiving a second printing.

The drawings of the heroines in the manga are so charming. I'm always looking forward to updates. I hope that anyone who hasn't read the manga yet will take this opportunity to check it out.

In addition to this book, I'm also writing an *isekai* fantasy called *Drugstore in Another World*. It's even going to be adapted into an anime! Unlike this series, that one is a slow-paced comedy about everyday life. If you feel like you've had enough serious *isekai* fantasy, then please give *Drugstore in Another World* a try. I recommend it.

I'm also currently writing a romcom. It's titled *The Girl I Saved on the Train Turned Out to Be My Childhood Friend*. The name is pretty long, and I always feel like I've messed it up whenever I mention it. The story is a straightforward young-love romcom without many perverse elements in it. If you'd like to read in another genre, why not pick it up?

Although I'm writing in many different genres, I really do like all of my series, and they all fit perfectly within my interests. I love all the characters, and I hope that I can continue exploring them.

Thank you for following all the way to the fourth volume. As mentioned, the next one will be very entertaining, so I hope you're excited.

Kennoji